ABOUT THE AUTHOR

Hugh Todd has lived in North London for over twenty-five years. He has had several stories published, including *One in 300,000,000* which was shortlisted for the Winston Fletcher prize. He is an award-winning copywriter and creative director and is the co-founder of the popular Behind the Billboard podcast. He gets his ideas from daily walks with his dog, Poppy, in his local park, so it's no surprise that is where his debut novel *It Happened in Clissold Park* is set.

IT HAPPENED IN CLISSOLD PARK

Hugh Todd

Troubador Publishing Ltd
Unit E2 Airfield Business Park,
Harrison Road, Market Harborough,
Leicestershire LE16 7UL
Tel: 0116 279 2299
Email: books@troubador.co.uk
Web: www.troubador.co.uk

ISBN 978-1-80514-333-8

British Library Cataloguing in Publication Data.
A catalogue record for this book is available from the British Library.

Printed and bound by CPI Group (UK) Ltd, Croydon, CR0 4YY
Typeset in 11pt Minion Pro by Troubador Publishing Ltd, Leicester, UK

For Rachel, aka Joan

"I congratulate the inhabitants of North London on having secured for their use forever 53 acres of the most beautiful park in the neighbourhood of the metropolis."

Joseph Beck, 1888

JANUARY

An audience of one

Lloyd unlocked the large iron gate and walked reluctantly into the park, careful not to slip on the icy pathway. For the next five days this was home, or rather work, as he was doing five morning shifts in a row. He passed the frosted bronze statue of Lord Clissold and gave him a polite nod: "Morning, squire."

First stop was the bins by the two large ponds at the north end of the park. He stopped the electric buggy by the railings, the wheels forcing a crunch from the fresh carpet of snow. He adjusted his large black Rasta hat, replacing a couple of greying dreadlocks that had escaped, before leaning across the seat for his trusty litter-picker stick. Then he got to work reaching for a ketchup-stained PFC takeaway box, fumbling for a moment, edging the carton along the frozen path towards the pond railings. As he grabbed it at the second attempt, something caught his eye: a glint from a shiny surface. For a minute his heart raced, and he wondered if it was a knife, maybe something to do with the moped gang? Instinctively he looked around, but at 7am on a January morning Clissold Park was desolate. Lloyd the park-keeper was the only soul in there, with just wildlife for company.

He knew every inch of the place. The drug dealers' bench. The reeds where the cygnets hatched. The divot by the under-elevens' penalty spot. That's what came from spending your childhood in the park. His family had settled in the area when he was a kid, swapping the beaches of Jamaica for the grasses of Clissold Park. The place had seemed enormous back then. Lloyd and his two younger brothers testing their mother's patience, playing hide-and-seek for hours after school. Lloyd's favourite spot had been just beyond the ponds, in a hollowed-out tree in the woodlands. To this day, he'd never told his brothers about it. As well as knowing the geography of the place, Lloyd knew the locals too. He was on nodding terms with all the mums and dads, runners, dog walkers and oddballs you get in a park.

But this discovery had thrown him. Shivering in his regulation green overalls, which he swore were thinner than a Rizla paper, he checked his footing on the frozen pathway before leaning over the railings to get a better look.

He pushed back the tall, stiff reeds, tiny splinters of ice flicking in his face, to reveal not a blade, but a pair of pristine white ice skates lying neatly on their side. He felt a wave of relief, before reaching down to pick them up. They were still warm inside. He looked up sharply, panicking a nearby moorhen, and saw a figure dashing across the zebra crossing just outside the park gates. His interest piqued, his heart rate rose, and he could hear the blood pounding in his ears.

He chucked the black bin bags into the back of the buggy, before carefully placing the skates on the passenger seat next to him. He adjusted his hat in the mirror, pulling the peak down a touch, and drove off, retuning the radio from Capital to Radio 2. 'Let's Face the Music and Dance' was playing. Lloyd hummed along; the music reminded him of his time dancing and acting at Hackney Youth Theatre, where he had been lauded for his poise and grace. The moves had long since left him, but the music remained close to his heart.

He adopted a straight-arm driving pose, like some TV cop on a case, needing to get to the bottom of this mystery. He looked over at the skates: *Do they belong to the figure racing across the road? Why haven't I seen them before? And how do I keep this secret from Rob 'by the book' Brown?*

Lloyd stooped his tall frame and entered the musky wooden hut, hat gently nudging the naked light bulb. He could still see his breath, but at least he was out of the cold and could warm up with a brew and a drop of rum. He filled the kettle and spotted the work schedule on the cupboard door: 'Lloyd all week!' scrawled in red felt-tip, and a smiley face. He could hear Rob laughing as he'd scribbled it.

Normally they took it in turns who worked the Monday morning shift and then alternated for the rest of the week, but with Rob staying home every morning all week for the builders, Lloyd was working earlies for the next five days.

He savoured his sweet alcoholic tea and enjoyed being in the shed on his own. When Rob was in there, it felt loud and crowded. At times, it all got too much and he would take himself over to Janet's shed by the reindeer pen. Janet was the park vet who looked after the animals. She was the opposite of Rob: serene, relaxed, easy to be around. Her shed was an oasis of calm, which Lloyd loved.

He resolved not to tell Rob about the skates. It would only set him off on another trail of worry. Lloyd was fond of Rob. He thought he was decent, he did a good job, but the fussiness was too much. He always seemed to be fretting about something: the holes in the perimeter fence, the stray tennis balls left on the courts, even the angle the kettle faced when they went out on their rounds had to be just right. And he had an unhealthy obsession with lost property.

Lloyd looked up at the clock before swigging the rest of the tea. He got into the buggy and headed back out. He was going to take the skates back to where he'd found them.

On his way, he took a detour to his beloved roses at the front of Clissold House. The four neat beds were his pride and joy, and he checked that the fresh compost he'd covered them with last week had settled.

The rest of the day was fairly uneventful, other than bumping into one of the park's regular dog walkers, Keith, and his cockapoo, Poppy. The extreme weather was down to what the weathermen were calling 'Ice Storm Ivan' blowing in from Russia. Lloyd called it something else, some parts of him still only just warming up. But if his body was slow coming to life, his mind was going faster than ever. He couldn't stop thinking about the skates.

As he left the park, he was tempted to double back to the pond and check they were still there, but the school kids were having fun in the snow, and it seemed

4

unnecessary. He'd placed them back exactly where he'd found them, as if they were a pair of newly hatched chicks, ensuring full cover was given by the nearby reeds.

As an extra touch, he'd covered the blades with a bit of foliage. *Don't want another nosy park-keeper finding them, do we?* He'd spotted his little feathered friend, the moorhen, and put his finger to his lips.

***

The next morning, he went straight to the pond and hid behind the bins. Anyone passing would have thought he was acting out some bizarre game of hide-and-seek. He looked an incongruous figure, crawling on his stomach SAS-style alongside the pond railings. The cold cut through his uniform, but not to his skin. He felt a moment of warm satisfaction at his decision to wear leggings.

Lloyd crept up to the reeds and gently pushed them aside. The skates weren't there. The moorhen scuttled away from its nest as he looked down. His heart started to race.

At first nothing happened, and he wondered for a horrible moment if Rob had somehow found the skates and they were now sitting neatly in their shed in the lost property box. But then he heard it. Muffled and distant at first, the *swish-swish* of steel on ice, getting closer by the second. There was a rhythm to it, hypnotic.

He looked up and saw a neat female figure moving gracefully across the frozen pond. She seemed to be magnetically attached to the surface. With every move, she was seeking out more of the ice, hands in the small of her back, swerving in front of the bulrushes. A nearby duck flapped its wings. The sound of blade on ice growing harsher as the skates carved ever sharper turns, then returning to larger, quieter arcs, before the silence of a single graceful glide, like a majestic swan.

Lloyd was transfixed, enthralled, and worried all at once. His brain was struggling to deal with so many emotions so early in the day at such a low temperature. He thought about filming her on his phone, but remembered he'd left it in the buggy. So, he recorded her movements onto his brain's hard drive instead. Like a ballerina with great poise and grace, she continued the show, skating behind the huge clump of trees in the centre of the pond, momentarily hidden from view.

He looked down and checked himself: damp patches on both knees, but nothing had penetrated through to his skin. Even if he had been soaked it wouldn't matter. He didn't care about his five early shifts in a row or Ice Storm Ivan or charging the buggy or any of those dull things that normally filled his mind. Nothing else mattered but this moment. This was better than – *Oh, here she is again!*

It was hard to get a look at her face in the semi-darkness of the early hour, with the hoodie tied close to her head. But suddenly the arcing headlights of a passing bus lit up her features for a moment: small, neat nose, pale skin adorned with freckles, and a rosebud mouth. Her steely blue eyes were totally lost in the moment, with no idea that Lloyd, the fifty-year-old park-keeper hiding in the reeds opposite, was also totally lost in the moment.

She came closer, much closer, before a hard stop not six feet away. Tiny shards of ice kicked into the air, landing on his face, his large, brown eyes blinking away the frosty flecks. He was so absorbed he hadn't realised she'd end up being this close. And he certainly hadn't figured on having ice flicked in his face. He daren't look, petrified he'd be discovered.

The moorhen came to his rescue, flapping its wings and skidding on the ice, distracting the girl as she carefully removed the skates and popped on her trainers. She placed the skates next to the nest without looking around, convinced she was alone, unaware she had just put on a faultless show for an audience of one. She double-checked the skates were well hidden behind the reeds and was up over the black iron railings and across the zebra crossing in a matter of seconds.

Lloyd's heart was still racing. He looked over at the skates to ensure they were properly hidden, leaving no evidence of the show that had just taken place, before heading back to the shed, celebrating with a tiny slide along the icy pathway.

The rest of the day was spent somewhat in a daze. Lloyd couldn't stop thinking about what had happened. And how he was the only person in the entire park to have witnessed the event. He left the park that evening with a spring in his step, and thoughts of fried chicken.

***

"Here he is! Lloyd, the lord of the manor!" Deji leant across the pristine white counter and gripped Lloyd's outstretched palm.

"Alright, Deji," replied a smiling Lloyd, pleased to be in the warmth of KFC. "I've been thinking about this all afternoon."

"Well, I'm pleased to hear you've had a good day, old man."

Deji was cheeky, but in a fun way, never nasty. Working the counter at KFC was his first job since leaving school and he seemed to be revelling in the role, his natural banter going down well with the locals. Lloyd knew Deji and his sister, Abi, from the estate near the park and loved the chat. And now they were even more connected through their love of fried chicken.

"Yeah, it's been a good day for sure," Lloyd replied, the skater momentarily gliding through his mind.

"There's no better way to celebrate a good day than with 'The Colonel'. A mighty fine choice. What you after?"

Lloyd smiled at Deji's impish young face, bright eyes full of life, before looking up at the vast offerings from the menu overhead. If he could afford it (and if his body would take it), he'd be in here every night. So much choice. So much delicious chicken.

"Chicken Zinger Meal Deal please, Deji, with all the extras."

Deji's eyes grew bigger: "Now that *is* a good day, coming right up."

Within minutes, the sweet-smelling bag of takeout food was handed over.

"Enjoy, my man."

"Cheers, Deji."

As Lloyd left, he spotted a moped parked out front.

"Those your new wheels?" he asked.

"You know it," replied a proud Deji.

"That must've been a lot of overtime, bro." Lloyd whistled in admiration at the black moped which had a distinctive 'DJ' tag on the back of the seat. "You keep it safe now. Don't want no moped gang stealing that, you hear?"

***

For Lloyd, this was a good moment and it needed marking. He remembered from his days at Stoke Newington School, his favourite dinner lady, Mary, always used to say, "Enjoy the good days, Lloyd, because there'll be a bad one just around the corner." She'd been so good to him when they'd first arrived. He often got into trouble, but she was always there, offering a kind word or a hand to hold. Mary knew what it meant to arrive on these shores from a foreign land, having come to England herself from Belgium before the war. She would always tell people with pride that she was from Belgium. Her mother had said, "You need to be proud of your background, your heritage. Stand up for yourself." It soon became Mary's mantra that she used for just about any sticky situation. *Why do you talk so much? Why are you so loud? Why is there so much cream on your pudding?* All were answered with the same enigmatic reply – "It's the Belgian in me!" – followed by a great roar of laughter.

Mary had passed away last year but Lloyd would never forget her. Whenever there was a moment of celebration, she came to mind. And in front of him was quite a celebration: burger, wings, fries, coleslaw, ketchup and

Coke topped up with a splash of rum, to be enjoyed while watching *A Place in the Sun* and then another favourite, *Antiques Roadshow*. Simple pleasures enjoyed in the one-bedroom flat he shared with Queenie, who got to clean up the box, nosing it around the vinyl flooring, before settling on his lap, purring over the sound of the television.

The news was full of the war in Ukraine and the energy crisis, and said the freezing conditions of Ice Storm Ivan were set to continue. Lloyd put his boots under the radiator and uniform on top. He was already looking forward to tomorrow.

***

The next performance was even better than the first. Lloyd was more organised this time and got settled in position nice and early. Even the moorhen seemed to know the drill and managed to sit quietly a few feet away, cleaning its feathers before the curtain went up. She arrived like yesterday, same outfit – black hoodie and leggings offset by the white skates.

She was once again lit by the intermittent arcing headlights from the road, but today there was also some top lighting coming from the council flats overlooking the pond, the early risers adding a touch of ambient glow to the arena below. Lloyd pulled the peak of his hat as far down as it would go, his dreadlocks squeezed tight to his scalp, and zipped up his jacket over his chin and nose, allowing just a slit for vision.

As she sped across the ice it wasn't only Lloyd and his feathery sidekick she enchanted. The wildlife on the opposite side of the pond seemed to appreciate the show too. A couple of geese had decided to stop hissing for a moment, craning their slim white necks to get a view of this curious visitor to their habitat.

She executed several new moves today: slaloming through a series of sticks and skating backwards in circles around a large plastic bottle. A show of skill and grace. Lloyd wanted to clap out loud, not just to warm his hands but to applaud another amazing spectacle.

Lloyd became so engrossed in the performances he started to mark them in his head and recall his favourite moves. So far, the slalom was the best, a perfect 6.0. Last night he'd secretly chucked a couple of rogue sticks onto the pond to increase the factor of difficulty, but she seemed to relish the extra challenge, zigzagging through the knobbly branches with ease.

Towards the end of the week, he couldn't contain himself any longer and did the thing he'd said he wouldn't do. He wrote her a note and stuffed it in her skate. As he watched her the next morning, he felt embarrassed and silly, and wished he'd never written it. Why on earth would she be interested in his dancing from all those years ago?

He looked down and noticed a few white specks around the edges of the moorhen's nest. He pulled at one. It was a chewed piece of paper. He inspected further and realised the moorhen had sabotaged his efforts to contact the skater, using his note as extra lining for her nest. Lloyd shook his head, relieved.

"Thank you, my dear," he whispered, heading back to the hut.

At the weekend crossover of shifts, Rob had news: "Have you seen them? On the pond?" Rob's face was scrunched up in annoyance that someone could dare to break the rules of the park. Lloyd stayed silent and looked at the chipboard floor, butterflies in his stomach.

"I can't believe you've not seen them," continued Rob, sipping from his Arsenal mug, "big cut marks, like somebody's been ice skating on the pond."

Lloyd readjusted his hat and rubbed the back of his neck. Rob was on a roll, his voice loud and more indignant. "We can't be having that. If I catch them, they'll know about it."

Lloyd summoned his old acting skills.

"What? No idea what you're talking about. Skating? It could be anything. Sticks scratching the ice, the geese, swans, God knows."

But Rob was adamant, putting his mug down firmly on the side. "Nah, mate, I'm telling you, something's up."

It chilled Lloyd's bones. He knew what Rob was like. Once he got his teeth into something, he never let go. And his teeth really were something to behold, so many of them, so white, it was a wonder how they all crammed into his mouth.

Lloyd looked down at a rip in his uniform trousers and picked at the leggings underneath, waiting for Rob to leave. Lloyd turned the radio up. There was news of the weather. The thaw had begun. By the end of the weekend, it would be edging above zero. Lloyd's shoulders drooped and he felt colder than ever.

Lloyd had the next Monday morning off. He stretched and looked out of the window and realised after a moment that something was different. The snow had melted. The magic had gone, leaving just the ugly skeleton of Clapton for all to see.

He slumped back to bed before doing something he'd never done before: he texted Rob to check everything was OK. He got an instant reply: BEEN AN INCIDENT AT THE POND. SPEAK LATER.

***

Lloyd thought his heart was going to explode out of his chest as he raced across the park. The whole of his upper torso was heaving up and down as if he was having a seizure, but somehow, he still remembered to swerve the divot by the under-elevens' penalty spot.

As he got closer, he spotted an ambulance by the pond and slowed a little. An area had been cordoned off and somebody was being treated on a stretcher. He saw Rob.

"Is she OK? Please, Rob, tell me she's OK."

"Yeah, of course she's OK," replied Rob, half laughing. "Stupid mutt! She was chasing a stick and went through the ice. She got out no problem. Can't say the same for Keith, poor bugger, he's really done his ankle. Lucky I was doing the rounds. Had to drag him out all by myself."

Lloyd adjusted the peak of his hat and mumbled: "OK yeah. Hope Keith's OK. Got to go." He wandered off sheepishly past the pond and looked over at the reeds.

Rob broke off from dealing with the paramedic and shouted, "Lloyd, who did you think it was, mate?" But Lloyd was out of earshot.

At the gate, Lloyd turned for one last look at the pond and wondered if it had really happened. The cold can do funny things to an old, slightly rum-addled mind. Was the skater a figment of a nostalgic brain? Or was she to be one of his greatest park secrets?

The moorhen sat in its nest and looked across the pond. A melting fragment of ice with carved blade patterns sank under the dismal grey waters.

FEBRUARY

Romeo & Juliet and Ali

Josh saw her across the park. Like he did every day. And every day prior to this one, she'd ignored him. But today was going to be different. He'd been practising the greeting with his friend Ali from the Turkish shop. The trick was putting the emphasis on the second syllable.

She approached. Her face hard, beautiful. The pink tracksuit soft, cosy. His heart racing. *'Don't blow it, Romeo!'* Ali's voice ringing in his ears. It was now or never.

"Günaydın," he said. She smiled. A big, beautiful, genuine smile. And walked past, trying not to react to the surprisingly well-pronounced greeting.

He'd done it. He'd said, "Good morning." And best of all, she'd finally noticed him.

***

Josh strode into the Arsenal Mini Market on Blackstock

15

Road feeling ten feet tall. Ali looked up, a smile growing across his face as he leant back on his rickety stool.

"Aye aye – Romeo's back! How was it?"

"Yeah, good," replied Josh, confidently.

"Did you get the pronunciation right?"

"Yep. 'Good-*night*-in'?"

"*Günaydın*… perfect."

Ali was full of pride, as if Josh were one of his own. A bit of a stretch seeing as Josh was six foot tall and pale as a ghost, with fiery Ed Sheeran hair and not an ounce of fat on him.

"So, what next, Romeo?"

"I was about to ask you the same question, Ali."

Ali put his worry beads down for a moment and rubbed his stubbly chin, gazing at the shelf opposite, as if a maxi pack of Hula Hoops was going to give him inspiration.

"Golden Virginia please, Ali." The moment was broken by Mick the janitor from Cally City Farm, who was one of Ali's regulars. Ali turned to the bank of cigarettes behind him and grabbed a pack of rolling tobacco.

"There you go, Mick. Say hello to the pigs for me."

Mick chuckled. "Will do."

Ali turned his attention back to Josh, large brown eyes surveying the young apprentice.

"OK, Romeo, let's talk."

***

Josh had realised early on that without classic good looks or any kind of muscle definition (his nickname at school was 'The Rake'), he needed a more considered approach to ingratiate himself with the opposite sex. And for that he had turned to his local shopkeeper, Ali.

They'd struck up a strong friendship over the years, starting with Josh popping in for sweets and treats on his way home from school. Josh trusted Ali. A male figure to look up to, someone who was always there for him (during opening hours, at least), unlike his dad, who'd left when he was twelve. Josh had felt lost for a few years and got sucked in by Matt and his moped gang, who he still couldn't quite shake. But he was hoping this romance could be the start of better things.

If he timed his run well (Tuesday mornings were best) he could get a good ten minutes with the big man, learning 'The Art of Romance – an exclusive one-to-one course hosted by local shopkeeper and Turkish translator, Ali'.

***

Josh approached Clissold Park with a mix of giddy excitement and anxiety. He entered through the large, black metal gates and looked up at the statue of Lord Clissold and his ridiculous coiffured hair. Josh instinctively pulled his fringe down a little, checking it wasn't doing that sticky-up thing.

He spotted her by the fountain, remembering this exact same scenario from a few weeks back, when she would walk past and ignore him. Now she was walking directly up to him, slightly pigeon-toed in her pristine Nike Air Force 1s. Same soft tracksuit, same million-dollar smile. He couldn't quite believe it.

She caught him checking his appearance before he had time to hide his phone, his pale cheeks flushed to match his hair. She didn't seem to notice. Or care.

"Come on, let's go." And just like that, they wandered off arm in arm, as if they'd been doing it all their lives.

They walked under the two enormous trees by the gates. The trees had been there as long as Josh could remember: big, solid, protective – a bit like Ali. In the spring, their branches were heavy with leaves, drooping down and offering cover for all sorts of nefarious activities. Josh remembered having his first cigarette here with Matt. But he desperately didn't want to think of Matt or mopeds or gangs right now.

He just wanted her.

They walked towards the ponds on the north side of the park, hands cold by their sides, occasionally brushing against each other, the merest touch sending waves of electricity up Josh's arm. He was trying to play it cool, as if he always walked around Clissold Park with one of the hottest girls in Stoke Newington beside him. *Imagine if we kissed*, he thought. *Or got naked*. Josh thought he might well explode if this happened.

At the ponds, they sat on Dennis Hickley, 19th August 1919–27th January 2015 'Keen birdwatcher who loved the ponds' and gazed across the water which, up until a few weeks ago, had been frozen solid by Ice Storm Ivan. They threw the odd stone into the pond, teasing the ducks into thinking they were being fed.

Eleven o'clock seemed the perfect moment. The sun had had time to defrost the park, and the early morning rush of dog walkers and runners, followed by the dash of parents and kids to school, had all but passed. They spotted Lloyd, the friendly park-keeper, doing his rounds in the green buggy. They'd seen him quite a bit these past few weeks and he always gave them a nod and a smile. They much preferred him to the other one with the baby face and blond hair who was always going on about keeping the park tidy, like some nagging old lady.

They scrolled TikTok for a bit, laughing at Josh's favourite clip of a man running in enormous bunny slippers. She flicked her hair out of her face to give him the full-beam smile. She was genuinely happy for the first time in months. Josh was exactly what she needed right now. And she was very much what he needed too.

As they went their separate ways, she reminded him her name was spelt with a double 's', so he could find her on Instagram. "Essen," she said to him, looking directly into his baby-blue eyes. He said it back softly, nodding, unable to hold her glance, shyly looking down at his scruffy Vans. She gave him a wink and giggled as he tried to wink back, half-shutting both his eyes by mistake.

He crossed the road out of the park, nearly getting knocked over by a Deliveroo bike. "Watch where you're going, you lanky prick!" Smiling, Josh waved at him in apology.

***

Walking and sitting on benches soon turned into snogging and groping under trees and anywhere they could find a secluded spot. Clissold Park became their home ground. Although, one day, Josh did manage to

19

persuade Essen to take in the delights of the Emirates football stadium.

Being a Gooner, it was heaven for Josh, walking with his beautiful girl round his beloved Arsenal stadium. They read the stories on the walls before a prolonged kissing session underneath the enormous mural of Thierry Henry. Josh opened his eyes mid-snog and peeked at his 100-feet tall hero towering over them. He couldn't wait to tell Ali.

On their way out, they took a couple of selfies with Herbert Chapman, draping their arms around the statue of the legendary Arsenal manager, squeezing their faces into the frame. Josh was hoping to persuade Essen to come with him into the Armoury Shop so he could buy her a Gunnersaurus, but thought that might be pushing his luck.

***

Josh walked in with a swagger, checking there were no customers about, before standing in front of Ali, arms folded, nodding as if he was Bukayo Saka having just scored in front of sixty thousand delirious Arsenal fans.

"I sense good news?" enquired Ali.

"Oh yes," replied Josh emphatically.

"What's the latest? How many dates you been on?"

Josh totted them up.

"Four."

"What was best?"

"Easy. Today. Just came back from the Emirates."

Ali raised his thick brown eyebrows and rubbed his bald head.

"The Emirates? You took the potential love of your life to a football stadium?"

"Yeah, it was sick. We kissed right under Henry."

Ali's sarcastic tone clearly hadn't landed. *That's the power of love*, he thought.

"So, did she enjoy it? Walking around a football stadium?"

"Yeah, think so."

Ali lent forward and whispered in conspiratorial fashion: "She's not a Spurs fan, is she?"

Josh laughed and shook his head.

"No way! Never! To be honest, I'm not sure if she's that into football. I was telling her about The Invincibles season, and she went on her phone for a bit."

"That's fine, mate. I reckon it's time for the next stage."

"What next stage?" asked a quizzical Josh.

"Well, let's see. You've done the walking, you've done the talking and some of the other, I imagine, so now it's time to get in the kitchen and do some cooking."

Josh's soft red eyebrows were furrowed slightly.

"Cooking, Josh!" exclaimed Ali. "It's time to cook your Juliet a meal. Give this romance a bit of depth and flavour."

Ali slipped off his throne, the creaky white stool getting some welcome relief. He wandered over to the front of the shop and shouted out to his brother, Yucel, in Turkish to watch the till for a minute.

Ali caressed an onion as if it were some precious stone, his enormous olive-coloured hands making it seem more like a pebble than a 'large Spanish'.

"These aren't just any onions, Romeo, these are spheres of love that will bring tears of joy to both you and your Juliet this Valentine's Day." Ali was in his element, describing the onions in his best impersonation of an M&S advert.

"Can't I just take her to Tetto's?"

"No! You want to blow her socks off, right? And the rest? It's the finest gesture of love to make something with your own hands. Plus, you could never afford Tetto's, especially on Valentine's Day."

Ali threw his young acolyte a head of garlic. "You'll need this and one of these." He slapped an aubergine into the lad's hand. They both looked at the dark, gleaming phallus on Romeo's pale palm and giggled like schoolboys.

"Seriously though, salt it first, takes the bitterness out. Then pour in some chopped tomatoes and the finishing touch." Ali's hand reached under the counter and patted around, first touching the baseball bat – *Nope don't need that today* – before finding a small, clear bag.

"Saffron, mate. The clincher." The delicate flame-coloured spice matched Josh's hair.

"Cheers, Ali. And how about some booze. This any good?"

Josh reached up and grabbed a bottle of red wine from the shelf, revealing a pair of large, black bolt-cutters in his back pocket, the type that can snip through a graphite lock like a knife through butter. It was the weapon of choice of the local moped gang who'd been stealing virtually every bike in the area.

Ali froze. *Shit, have I got this kid all wrong?* His mind started to race: the story in the *Islington Gazette*, the moped gang, the increasingly violent attacks.

Was Romeo not who he thought he was?

Ali shifted uneasily on his stool, looking down at the counter, hand now twitching above the baseball bat, not wanting to look Josh in the eye anymore.

Josh paid for the food and laughed as he left. "I love you, mate!"

Ali slumped and stared at the back of Josh's head.

Who is Juliet, he thought, *and how do I warn her?*

"You alright, Ali?" asked a warm voice. "You look like you've just seen a ghost."

Ali looked up to see Janet, the park vet, place a large bag of oats on the counter.

"Sorry, Janet, miles away."

***

Essen ran the brush through her thick, dark hair, parted in the middle, hanging like long, velvet curtains on either side of her bold, beautiful face. She checked in the mirror that both flanks were equal. She absentmindedly examined a few split ends and thought about all the other boyfriends she'd had before Josh. And how absolutely crap they'd all been. Good-looking, ripped, tossers.

It was like she'd had to kiss all those princes before she got her frog. She didn't *not* fancy Josh. It was just he was different. Not a cliché, or somebody trying to be something they weren't.

From the day he'd summoned up the courage to say 'good morning' in her mother tongue she'd been hooked. That took some balls. She liked that. And she'd take it any day over a chiselled jaw or pumped bicep. Plus, she'd always had a soft spot for Ed Sheeran.

And now here they were. Onto their next date, dinner at his to celebrate Valentine's Day. Just the thought of it made her smile. She dabbed a drop of perfume behind her ears, one last pout in the mirror, and off she went.

***

Josh had been brought up by his mum, along with his two younger siblings. Dad had left when they were young, which had made life hard for them all. Mum had worked three part-time jobs to cover the family expenses. As a result, Josh had had long periods on his own, either playing PlayStation or hanging out with mates. He'd been easily led astray, especially by Matt and his moped gang.

At first, Josh had thought being in the gang was a bit of fun – get a bit of street cred and maybe girls would find him more attractive. But things had escalated recently, and it had gone from sitting on the back of Matt's moped, racing up and down Highbury Barn, to something much worse. Matt had started carrying a claw hammer and demanded Josh get more involved, forcing the bolt cutters on him, making Josh cut the locks from the stolen mopeds. These acts could get Josh sent to jail. He hated it and knew he had to get out. Meeting Essen was the perfect excuse, and he'd decided to get out. A week ago, he had told Matt he was leaving.

***

Cooking Valentine's dinner for the most beautiful girl in the world took Josh's mind away from thoughts of the gang. He focused on the food as he tried to remember what Ali had told him. The onions seemed to be the easy bit, as were the tins of tomatoes, but the aubergines were something else.

Did he peel them or slice them? Boil or fry them? He hadn't a clue, and didn't have the time to run down to the shop for advice. He cut them up into chunks and threw them into the pan with everything else, hoping it would work.

He needn't have worried. The evening was a resounding success. Ali's aubergine, onion and saffron special worked a treat and Essen nodded as she ate. "This is good," she said with genuine surprise. "Reminds me of a family meal we have at the weekends."

They felt sophisticated, even if they were sipping their red wine in half-pint glasses. It was another moment that drew them closer together and the concrete-hard aubergine became a funny focal point, with Essen asking if the recipe had included cooking 'small rocks'.

For Essen, Josh going the extra mile again, trying to cook a special meal, made her realise how lucky she was to be with her curious blue-eyed boy.

***

Josh was a bag of nerves. He'd given this moment even more thought than all those days when he'd been trying to say hello to Essen. That seemed like a lifetime ago. And here he was about to meet her dad for the first time. Having not had his own father around for years, Josh wanted to make the right impression. He'd always somehow felt he was to blame for his dad leaving, so today was a chance, however small, to try and put that right. He knew Essen had a strong relationship with her dad and he wanted to respect it and prove to both of them he was good and decent.

As he approached the park, he spotted Lloyd getting ready to lock up for the night.

"Alright, Lloyd."

"Evening, young man," answered Lloyd. "Looking smart tonight. You off to see your fancy woman?"

"Yeah," said Josh tentatively. "Meeting her dad for the first time."

"Getting serious then," Lloyd replied. "Good luck. She's a lovely girl."

For a moment, the headlights from a passing bus lit a park bench, one of the many they'd sat on these past few weeks. Josh reread the caption engraved on the brass plaque: 'Richard "Dickie" Edwards, 4th July 1918–13th July 1940. Spitfire pilot who fought for his country in the Battle of Britain. He loved this park'. They'd chatted about 'Dickie' and wondered if he'd had a secret love in the park. They both hoped they might have a plaque somewhere for themselves one day.

He turned at the sound of a beep and saw a black moped driving past. It was Matt. They gave each other the middle finger and went their separate ways: Matt and his moped gang to more mayhem, Josh hopefully to a new life.

***

Essen beckoned him in, her smile lighting up the narrow hallway. She was about to introduce the man she loved to the man she loved: 'Dad meet Josh. Josh meet Dad.' She'd practised all afternoon while getting ready. And now the moment had arrived. Her freshly painted fingernails went in search of thumb skin to pick. She thought again how different this felt. Josh wasn't super-hot, but in a way, that was a relief. Pale skin, red hair, soft hands, every bit of him seemed unlike all the other dickheads. He respected her, was patient and knew the lyrics to 'Shape of You'. All of which qualified Josh to be the first invited into Dad's home.

The front room was classic Victorian terrace. The dark leather three-piece suite dominated proceedings, along with the flatscreen in the corner and the family portrait above the fire.

Josh walked in, but didn't sit down in case it was wrong, and looked at the back of the large figure down on his haunches, tending the fireplace. Essen walked across the rug and gently touched her dad on the shoulder.

"Dad, this is Josh. Josh, this is my dad." Her father stood up. The minute he rose, the room seemed to shrink. He was the biggest piece of furniture in there. He rubbed his bald head and prepared his trademark smile as he turned to welcome his guest.

Essen sensed something was wrong. *Why had he paused? Why wasn't Dad saying anything? Where was the chuckle; the big, outstretched hand; the offer of a seat? Nothing.*

She turned to Josh and, on his face, there was a look she'd never seen before. He'd gone white. He was nearly albino white as it was, but what little blood he had in his face seemed to have drained all the way down to his scruffy sneakers.

She heard her dad utter something, his face etched with confusion: "Romeo?"

Not three feet away, at the end of the sofa, Josh murmured: "Ali?"

Essen in the middle, like a boxing referee, stared from one to the other and back again, dumbfounded.

"Do you two know each other?"

MARCH

One in 300,000,000

Keith appeared in the kitchen like an overexcited child. Margaret was well used to it: fifty years of marriage did that. Her husband was a bundle of energy: lively, darting eyes, cheeky smile, greeting the dog much like the dog greeted him, joy and devotion in equal measure. Another marriage made in heaven. Even after the terrible news in January, Keith still seemed to have a spring in his step. Margaret knew he was having a tough time, but he was remarkable in his outlook, and she loved him even more for it.

He peered out of the window at the clear, blue skies, and she knew what was coming.

"Boston weather!" he exclaimed. A little nod from Margaret and a dutiful smile as he recalled his happy time in the States all those years ago. He zipped up his fleece, the rip by the elbow reminding Margaret of his accident on the pond on the same day he was diagnosed.

Hopefully things will be better after the hospital today, she thought. He pulled his flat cap down as far as it would go.

"Have you really got time for this, Keith? We've got to be there by 11.15."

"Yes, I know, love. But I need to. Don't fuss."

Their eyes met. Nothing more needed to be said. She reached over and gently took a bit of fluff from his fleece that had got caught in his beard. He nodded in thanks and said: "I'll be back by ten at the latest." He checked himself in the hallway mirror before shouting, "Come on, Poppy. Let's go!" And, with tails wagging, they were gone. The door slammed, a waft of cold air accompanying Margaret back into the kitchen as she glanced anxiously at the letter on the side. '*11.30am Whittington Blood & Bone Marrow Ward. Dr Emberton. Please report fifteen minutes before your appointment at main reception*'. She looked at her watch: 8.30am.

On days like today, she went into flapjack mode; anything to take her mind off the events ahead. The hospital had searched for months for a donor, but it turned out Keith's blood type was as unique as Keith himself. And myelofibrosis was a fiendishly rare bone marrow disorder.

She looked out into the back garden and saw a robin skid on the frozen bird bath. Keith was a little wobbly on the ice too. She was forever telling him to slow down, but he really had surpassed himself on the frozen pond that day, racing Poppy for a stick, breaking his ankle. Thank goodness that efficient park-keeper had acted so quickly. She had never been keen on him, always seemed a bit full of himself, but that all changed after he rescued Keith and pulled him from the freezing pond.

It had been awful for Keith, being on crutches – a test for the world's most energetic seventy-four-year-old – but worse, much worse, had been finding the presence of leukaemia during the routine blood tests.

"What are the chances?" Keith had murmured in the hospital.

As a statistician for nearly forty years, Keith was naturally fascinated by the probability of what had happened to him: going for a walk one morning, fit and healthy, and returning home with a snapped ankle and a potential death sentence. That day had been pretty surreal, with three sets of doctors giving Keith and Margaret the ever-worsening news. However, in some ways, the odds were in their favour: there was a chance he was going to be all right.

He could be treated with an allogeneic transplant that could give him another ten years. And that chance of survival was about to arrive today in the form of Joseph Esterhaus, a perfect match for Keith's bone marrow.

Margaret turned the oven on and got the ingredients ready: butter, oats, but no sugar. She'd run out of demerara. She glanced up at the kitchen clock. Plenty of time. She put her jacket on and popped over to see Ali at the shop. He was sure to take her mind off things.

***

"She doesn't half make a fuss." Keith's breath was visible in the crisp air as he chatted to Poppy like an old mate from work, rather than an overexcited cockapoo. Keith clapped his gloved hands together to get the circulation going, before executing a mini skid on the icy pavement, arms out as if he were a kid on the way home from school.

Even for someone permanently chirpy, Keith was hyper today. It was his way of dealing with things. Poppy looked at him with a cocked, furry head.

"Yer daft mutt."

Keith looked at the clear, blue skies overhead and thought, *Somewhere up there is Joseph*, and felt a rush of adrenaline. This was the first amazing day of the rest of his life.

They walked past the postbox, around the corner to 'squirrel alley' where Poppy was let off the lead to give chase. It was their routine and they both loved it. No words were said, or orders barked, and before long they were in the park.

They wandered through the gates and past the statue. "Top of the morning to you, Lord Clissold!" said Keith in a mock-posh accent. It wasn't quite his old stomping ground of the Yorkshire Dales, but Clissold Park still had all the necessary ingredients: big vistas, wooded walks and two ponds teeming with wildlife. Even the fresh poo on the pathway this morning didn't upset him. Normally he'd be cursing and bagging it up and muttering about the owner, but today was different. Today even the dog shit looked good.

As they made their way along the pathway, Keith spotted the park-keeper's buggy approaching and a familiar face at the wheel: his saviour from back in January.

"Morning, Rob. Amazing day."

Rob's face broke into a smile, his pristine white teeth dominating his boyish face.

"Alright, Keith? Nice to see you, mate. How's life?" Rob stopped the buggy and took his sunglasses off to get a better look at Keith, adjusting his blond fringe to ensure the side parting remained intact. "You OK without those crutches now? That must've been a right pain."

"Yes, all healed up now, thanks, Rob. Just happy to be out and about again."

Keith couldn't bear to tell Rob about the leukaemia and the donor and what a big day it was. Best keep it casual. It would only complicate things.

"Well, I've got to be off," said Rob. "Some little bugger has cut two new holes in the fence on the far side. But you look after yourself, mate, and make sure that daft dog of yours doesn't get you into any more trouble."

"Don't worry about me, Rob. I'm fine," replied Keith, thinking of the trouble he was in, which had nothing to do with the dog. "And thanks again for everything."

"Pleasure, mate."

There was a familiar sound from above: the dull roar from 30,000 feet. Keith looked up at the white scar cutting across the blue canvas and marvelled at life, both down here and up there, half-disbelieving he'd been given a stay of execution. *What were the chances?* It whirred round his mind again. The probability of finding a donor cried out to be calculated. Especially when they'd been told it was a particularly rare strain of leukaemia. He'd actually run a programme on some old software at home and found it was a one in 4,351,456 chance. A shiver went down his spine.

***

BA flight 159 from Boston to London City Airport was beginning its descent. Pressure in the cabin was increasing as the passengers were ushered back to their seats. The pressure was particularly intense for one passenger, Joseph Esterhaus in Seat 21C, who was possibly the most important cargo on the plane.

The tall, distinguished, white-haired academic had never envisaged being a bone marrow donor: in fact, he still found it quite odd, sitting here on a plane, over London, 3,500 miles from home. But after losing his great friend Miles to leukaemia, he'd known he would always want to do something to save another life.

This was the right thing to do, and his bone marrow was a perfect match to save a certain Keith Atwell in North London, so that was where he was heading right now. However, he first needed to head off to the toilet, cursing the dodgy airline food. He'd known the lasagne smelt strange the minute he'd peeled the aluminium lid off, and now it was working its way through his large intestine at pace. No stern words from an air hostess were going to get in his way.

"I'm sorry, sir, you'll have to wait until the plane has landed."

"Ma'am, this is an emergency."

He rushed past and squeezed his rangy frame into the tiny cubicle.

***

Some 30,000 feet below, Keith was sauntering through

the woodlands, savouring every moment, as Poppy raced around the undergrowth. Another equally lively dog was headed towards them. Keith knew the busy beagle nearly as well as Poppy, such was the frequency with which he'd seen him over the years. "Eric!" shouted Keith. The beagle looked up as Poppy tentatively started to smell his bottom.

Keith greeted Eric's owner, Astrid, in more polite fashion, with a friendly smile. "Morning, Astrid. Amazing weather."

"Oh, isn't it just?" replied Astrid, who was leaning against a tree, resting her sore hip. Keith didn't really want to talk, so nodded amicably and continued walking.

A bit further into the woodlands, Keith paused by a pink blossom tree and gazed at the dramatic burst of colour. He walked under the blush canopy and marvelled at the patterns of petals. 'Tree dandruff' seemed such a cheap and negative way to describe one of nature's greatest creations. How could it be aligned with an itchy scalp? What sacrilege! He saw it more like a piece of installation art from Mother Nature herself. 'The pink snowball tree' he'd heard a little girl call it the other day, which seemed much more apt.

He came to a standstill and just let himself become absorbed, closing his eyes for a moment, before reopening and looking again, this time seeing dewdrops clinging to the undersides of the branches like perfectly formed globes of mercury. On the branches above, the birds sang like their lives depended on it: parakeets, robins and blackbirds creating a deafening morning chorus. He barely needed to turn up his hearing aid.

Alongside the wonders of wildlife, there was much real life here too: skiving schoolkids puffing on weed like big shots, teenagers kissing under the cover of trees, and Polish tennis players practising their forehands and English swear words in equal measure.

Keith always embraced life; he had no time for moaners or lazy buggers. Life was for living. 'Get up and get on' was his motto, and these past few weeks he was appreciating life a whole lot more. The Whittington Hospital had found a match, and it made these walks even more important.

He was looking forward to his second round of life. *Will Joseph be the same in real life as his picture? Tall, bright, handsome. Maybe it'll rub off on me*, thought Keith. *But seriously, will it work?* He quickened his stride. *How can I ever pay Joseph back?*

His mind started to race a little, vowing to be Joseph's friend for life. *I'm going to visit him every Christmas*, he promised. *Well, a card at least. I'll start writing my memoirs, I'll book that trip to Hawaii and learn the foxtrot with Margaret.*

The plane continued to cut across the sky, the long white jet stream slowly dissipating to nothing. A growl brought Keith back to earth. He looked down, a stick at his feet.

"Sorry, Poppy, miles away." He threw the stick, his brain automatically calculating the parabolic arc required for it to clear the nearby hedge.

***

Joseph barely had time to settle on the toilet seat before his bowels emptied. He felt the keen relief of losing excess gases and more, before flushing.

The familiar whoosh sucked it all away at the touch of a button. However, he noticed a chorus of thuds from the toilet as he turned to wash his hands. He paused. He thought nothing of it until later. *Maybe the plane has got a bad stomach too*, he thought. He heard the muffled voice on the other side of the door:

"Sir, you really need to return to your seat now."

The Boeing was on one of its last trips after twenty-five years in service and 145,000 hours in the air. Like all 747s, it had an exemplary safety record, apart from occasionally suffering from hairline cracks in its sewage tanks that led to a build-up of sanitising blue liquid, water and traces of human excreta. Basically, a stinky freezing cocktail of shit, known in the aviation industry as 'blue ice'.

And this blue ice had been slowly developing on the outside of the plane as it flew across the Atlantic, with Joseph's toilet visit being the catalyst for a large-sized block to snap free from the fuselage and begin its fall to earth.

***

Keith rounded the top of the pond and headed up towards the highest point in the park, the raised hill behind the tennis courts.

***

Once released from the side of the plane, the blue ice started its rapid descent. As it sped through the clouds, the rising temperature caused it to become smaller, tighter and denser, intent on getting to earth at top speed, terminal velocity now reaching 500mph.

**

The temperature in the oven was 200 degrees as the flapjacks were browning. Margaret was at the top of the house, putting the washing out on the roof terrace. The cold but sunny weather was perfect for drying, and a welcome change from draping wet clothes over the radiators downstairs. The sunlight glinted off the side of a plane overhead. For a moment, she let go of her anxiety and decided that everything was going to be OK.

**

Faster and faster the blue ice fell, a tiny freezing asteroid, blistering through the sky.

**

Keith reached the apex of the hill and stood next to another glorious blossom tree, taking in the view – the tennis courts, the ponds, the trees, the joggers, the dog walkers: all life was here.

"Tell you what, Poppy, there's no better feeling. This really is gran—"

He never got the '–d' out. The deadly chunk of blue ice, weighing 12kg but shrunk to the size of a tennis ball, hit Keith plumb on the head. He didn't stand a chance. The crack of his head briefly alerted the tennis players to look over. Keith collapsed onto the grass verge, green poo-bags falling from his coat pocket.

Poppy had no idea what had happened but, after dropping her stick, scampered over to sniff the frozen excreta and pieces of Keith's skull. She started to bark as small white petals floated gently down onto the prone figure.

***

A couple of hours later, the front doorbell rang. *Oh, about time! Forgot your keys too*, thought Margaret as she stomped towards the front door. She was fuming: *Today of all days! I've told you so many times. Always the same!* The door opened to reveal not Keith, but a couple of police officers.

"Margaret Atwell?"

"Yes, that's me. What's happened? What's going on?"

"Can we come in please."

***

A few days later, Margaret met for a sombre chat with Dr Emberton, the specialist who'd been looking after Keith. Although it was now slightly irrelevant, he wanted to inform Margaret that Keith's final biopsy results had been re-evaluated and his leukaemia had in fact been far too advanced for the transplant to have worked.

Keith would never have been saved by Joseph. It was already too late. So, in effect, the bolt from the blue was some kind of mercy. Margaret took solace from this, knowing Keith had died doing what he loved, up there on the mound, breathing in the clean morning air, admiring all of life with his beloved dog by his side.

***

A week later the *Islington Gazette* claimed the probability of Keith being killed outright by Joseph's blue ice was one in 300,000,000.

APRIL

A view to die for

Jack and Frieda had been together for over two hundred years, which even in tree-years was quite impressive. Life had thrown so much at them: storms, floods, two World Wars, the long, hot summer of '76, Ice Storm Ivan in January and, most recently, a case of bleeding canker, from which they'd both thankfully recovered.

Every new challenge, every passing season, brought them closer together. They may have looked like a pair of gnarly old souls, but inside they felt like a couple of young saplings madly in love. To the locals, they were known as merely 'the big old trees by the gate', two enormous horse chestnuts listed as T6 and T7 on the council plans of Clissold Park, but beneath the grass and flowers and running track, it was another world. Here they thrived, thanks to a vast matrix of underground capillaries that enabled them to communicate, eat, drink, exchange fluids, share feelings and yes, even have sex.

The visitors to the park loved them as much as they loved each other, but for different reasons. Young couples carved crude hearts into their scaly bark in public displays of affection. The pretty Turkish girl and her Ed Sheeran lookalike boyfriend were the most recent beneficiaries using the trees' canopy for private moments. The trees often dipped their branches an inch or two to add more cover, shielding the young sweethearts from prying eyes.

Anxious millennials were big fans too, becalmed by the trees' size and strength. And on Sunday mornings, the Brazilians from Wood Green had their moment, twisting and turning tattooed bodies on the dipping elastic tied between the trunks, accompanied by the twang of the berimbau. Jack and Frieda would both subtly lean back a few inches to make the elastic extra taut and aid a successful crossing, resulting in a nice big tree hug. And of course, there was much appreciation from the waggy-tailed dogs, sniffing and peeing all over their broad trunks.

It said something that even after being cut, stabbed, tied up with elastic and pissed on every day, they were still the happiest couple in the park.

***

Charlie Bullock sat on the edge of his fake mahogany desk in the glass office, imagining he was the Wolf of Wall Street addressing a boardroom of city traders, rather than the three pale-faced muppets gathered in front of him, who were his entire workforce at Watsons Estate Agents.

"Well, there's only one thing on the agenda this morning, or rather two. These two." Charlie turned his computer screen to face the muppet chorus. "These trees are screwing things up for this office right now. We've had fifteen viewings at The Vistas and not one bite. Nothing. Everyone is saying the same thing: 'The view is spoiled by the trees'."

The trees hadn't seemed a problem when the flats had been going up in winter, their skeletal silhouettes never really interrupting the view. But now, dressed in their full spring foliage, they were two huge, verdant blots on Charlie's landscape.

He raised his eyebrows. "Any thoughts?" His three employees stared vacantly at the screen. Giles, the failed graduate, now failing estate agent, thought the trees looked quite magnificent, icons of his local park, but considered it inappropriate to share this with his irritated boss.

"Well?" Charlie's heartbeat was increasing; the sweats had started. Too much coke at the weekend. He slammed his mug down, coffee spilling onto the table. Their cue to exit. The commission from the sale of The Vistas was potentially huge and would cover his upcoming golf trip to Dubai. There was only one thing for it.

He called Terry. The Tree Assassin.

***

They were lucky. Two horse chestnut seedlings meeting at the right time in the right place. It was meant to be. They could have been stuck on a pavement outside the park, like the silver birches on Riversdale Road, trying to live amidst concrete slabs, tarmac, gas pipes and cables. Even the most cunning capillaries couldn't work their way round that lot.

They were blessed, and it was all thanks to Lord Clissold. He'd planted the trees when he'd originally acquired the park, to mark boundaries and bring topographical variation to what he liked to call his 'big garden', which he admired from the master bedroom in Clissold House.

These two horse chestnuts had been his favourite trees in the whole estate. He'd noticed their trunks naturally leant inwards, giving the impression they were a couple. They'd reminded him of his beloved spaniels, Jack and Frieda, who'd been the greatest of friends. When the dogs had passed away, he'd given their names to the trees.

***

Terry put his pint down, wiped his mouth with the back of his callused hand and made the kind of statement he'd been making in the Highbury Barn pub for the past twenty years. "We need someone new up front, someone who can hold the ball, a classic number nine."

Charlie had heard it all before: the players' names had changed, but the chat was the same. This was a ritual they both knew well and loved. He nodded. "Yeah, I agree, mate. Someone like Smudger Smith or Radford."

"Radford?" Terry laughed. "Now you're talking, I remember him…" And on it went.

Normally they would've looked an odd couple – Charlie Bullock, tall, clean-cut, in brogues and chinos, next to the stocky, unshaven Terry Payne in T-shirt and jeans – but this was match day, and any man could be chatting to any man, as long as it was about 'The Arse'.

They'd been doing it since school, and nothing was going to change now. Charlie picked up their empty pint pots and headed to the bar, wondering when the moment would arise to divert the banter away from centre forwards to the burning issue of the day: those bloody trees.

Terry checked his phone for any last-minute team news and glanced across the pub. He spotted Rob the park-keeper talking to Kenroy the cabbie, both regulars on match days. They loved the chat and would definitely have had a point of view regarding the need for a new striker, but the pub was too crowded, so they just gave each other a hopeful thumbs-up for the game.

Charlie settled the fresh pints down and reached into his jacket pocket, flashing the purple silk lining, placing a brochure in front of Terry:

'HIGHBURY VISTAS: LUXURY APARTMENTS AVAILABLE SUMMER 2024'

"Here we go, boasting again are we, posh boy?" Terry rolled his eyes comically. Still, he couldn't help but lean in to get a better look at the glossy cover.

Charlie folded it out flat before his opening salvo.

"Mate, I need a favour."

Highbury Vistas were 'the epitome of modern urban living' the blurb claimed. 'Beautifully styled, with open-plan spaces flooded with natural light, premium integrated ceramic hobs with brushed steel ovens and built-in microwaves'.

The brochure was full-on property porn, which kept Terry interested as Charlie tucked into the pork scratchings. Terry read aloud in mock grandiose fashion: "The penthouse apartments offer uninterrupted views across Clissold Park."

Charlie looked Terry directly in the eye: "Except the views *are* currently interrupted by two enormous bloody trees." Terry held Charlie's gaze and then smiled, taking a sip of his pint, and ever so subtly licked his lips.

"I think I know where you're going with this. 'The Vistas' with no vista." Terry's rapier wit was kicking in.

Charlie looked around for a moment, but there was no chance anyone could hear them: the pub was packed with Gooners loudly debating the Arsenal forward line, or maybe they'd moved onto the defence by now – either way, no one was listening. Terry had a glint in his eye. He always needed money, but it was the actual work he loved; to him, chopping down trees was like a gladiatorial battle.

"Leave it with me, mate."

***

Of course, as with all long-term relationships, Jack and Frieda had their ups and downs. Two hundred years is more than enough time in which to have the odd argument. Frieda often berated Jack that he was too greedy, sucking up way more nutrients from the topsoil than was fair, meaning Frieda's capillaries had to work harder and reach deeper for supplies. *No wonder he's taller than me,* she thought.

Conversely, Jack often thought Frieda was too kind to the kids who'd climb all over them, often breaking their falls with opportunely positioned branches. Jack thought the kids needed to learn the hard way and experience scrapes and bruises. Frieda felt she was only doing what Mother Nature wanted.

Their latest row was on one of their main topics of conversation: the weather. Jack, being taller and broader than Frieda, felt the elements first: the early morning sun on his bark, the first splashes of rain on his crown and the wind in all its variations. Storms were the biggest worry, causing lasting damage, often snapping large branches which took an age to regrow. Jack would always warn Frieda, giving her time to tighten her bark, push her expanded roots further into the soil and brace herself for what was to come. But, on this occasion, Jack had been dozing when the wind got up and Frieda, unprepared, had lost two of her biggest branches. Perhaps they weren't as sprightly as they thought. No tree lives forever.

***

Arsenal had drawn 3-3 with lowly Southampton, and sixty thousand grumpy Gooners were streaming out of the Emirates. The natives were restless. All except one, who was quietly grinning to himself in the April sunshine.

Throughout the game, Terry had been considering Charlie's proposal and realised he had a way in. He knew the local tree officer, Colin Jones, who seemed a solid member of the community with his horticulture degree from Plymouth and tidy cardigan from Next. But Terry had known for years he was dodgy, selling logs illegally from the back of his old Volvo in Epping Forrest. At £50 a bag, it was a nice little earner.

Terry had him by the balls, or rather by the logs. Colin didn't take well to Terry's subtly threatening phone call later that night, but if it meant getting Terry off his back for good, he was prepared to do it. Colin knew the trees had previously had a bout of bleeding canker and if he claimed the potentially fatal disease had returned, it could work.

It was a close vote, but Colin's meticulously written report swung it, along with the desire from some council members for a 'more aesthetically modern foliage' aka 'out with the old, in with the new'. A notice was placed on the trees to notify members of the public of their imminent removal. And a lynching date was set.

***

It seemed like any other day to them. Sunlight peeking across the park from behind St Mary's Church spire, squirrels tickling their trunks, parakeets darting from Jack to Frieda and back again. Early mornings were their favourite. With an empty park, they could subtly stretch the very ends of their branches towards each other and experience the most gentle but heartfelt touch with their hand-like leaves.

This fragile act was a pleasure only they knew; a gentle, life-affirming moment to start any day. They'd love it to last for hours if they had the chance, this gentle caress... but they were normally curtailed by the park-keepers doing their rounds, or the first jogger of the day.

Today was different. They weren't interrupted by an animal or a runner, but by a large white van driving directly into the park from Green Lanes and parking right next to them on the sloping verge.

***

Terry had his apprentice, Danny, marking out a 200-square-foot area on the field in front of Frieda with yellow-and-black hazard tape.

"Are we starting with T7?" asked Danny. Terry reached into the pocket of his cargo trousers and unfolded the death warrant. He nodded.

"Yep, that one first," he said, pointing at Frieda, "then we'll break for lunch and do the other one," pointing at Jack.

Danny continued with the prep, positioning the chipper and laying out the rigging ropes. Terry reached into the back of the van, grabbing his helmet and earmuffs. He paused for a moment, testosterone starting to pump around his capillaries before he fired up the chainsaw. The parakeets took flight at the metallic scream.

Frieda sensed something was wrong and rustled her leaves in alarm, but it didn't have much effect. Terry's specialist tree-surgeon boots had been designed to climb El Capitan in Yosemite Park if need be, so what chance did she have here in Clissold Park?

Jack was worried, receiving pulses from Frieda's capillaries at a frightening rate.

Terry climbed to the crown and strapped himself into the cradle position, from where he could start working methodically downwards: first the limbs, then the body. He squinted up at the sunny sky, a vast blue canvas cut by a single jet stream.

Frieda's elegant, elongated limbs were severed one by one. The pain was excruciating. Terry had adapted his saw and sharpened it with a square, not round, file, enhancing both velocity and sharpness of cut. Frieda didn't give up easily, desperately pumping out small clouds of leaf toxins. The dry, bitter chemical attacked the back of Terry's throat.

He started to choke, gasping for breath. He pulled up his visor, turned away from the tree, needing air. "You OK, mate?" shouted Danny, holding the rigging ropes below. Terry regained his breath, gave the thumbs-up and on the slaughter went, the limbs guided down by Danny's ropes, a mountain of bones on the grass verge.

Frieda's capillaries were fading. Her first panicked messages to Jack had been filled with pain and fear, but now there was only one message: goodbye.

It had been a lynching, a public humiliation, reducing her to a carcass in front of him. A life of two hundred years wiped out in under two hours. It didn't seem real. *Surely this is a bad dream?* thought Jack. But the silent and lifeless capillaries told the awful truth, and he knew deep down their life together was over.

***

"Go and get us a couple of tinnies, Danny," said Terry. "Then we'll start in on the other one." As Danny headed to the Turkish supermarket on Blackstock Road to get some beers, Terry stretched his legs before sitting down on Elizabeth Kelly, 9th October 1947–14th September 2018 'Travelled the world but this park was her favourite destination', and lit a cigarette. He took his time, savouring the nicotine rush with every drag.

Rob drove past in the buggy and shouted out: "Can't believe we bloody drew with Villa!" which Terry acknowledged, rolling his eyes. He returned to Frieda and stubbed his cigarette out on her stump.

To Terry it seemed an innocuous action, a full stop before cutting down the next tree, but it triggered something in Jack he'd never previously felt. Within seconds of the cigarette being extinguished on Frieda's stump, Jack's capillaries were filled with rage, swelling to three times their original size. It happened all over, from his sturdy trunk, all the way along his branches, to the very tips of his leaves: a powerful sensation racing through his network of capillaries that spelt imminent danger, as if his entire being was preparing for battle.

The biggest change was in his large primary roots, which expanded into huge, thick, cable-like tentacles, thrashing around underground like a mini earthquake. These were forces never previously experienced in the park's history. Not even the bombs from the Blitz had been this disruptive. The parakeets in Jack's upper branches took flight, and a passing dog walker struggled to contain an Alsatian trying to flee the park.

Jack felt strength like he'd never known. It was as powerful as his love for Frieda, and without warning, one of his thickest roots burst the surface and sprayed soil all over Terry's back.

Terry instinctively touched his neck, but his mind was elsewhere, thinking about the money and the chilled beers Danny was getting.

He stood up and was walking towards the van when his foot got caught in something. He looked down to see an enormous black root had formed a loop around his foot. Terry tried to wiggle his foot free, but after a moment, realised his boot was properly stuck.

As Terry struggled, Jack sensed he had a grip on his prey and started to squeeze his root more tightly around Terry's foot. He did it as slowly as possible, wanting the murdering tree surgeon to suffer like Frieda had.

The pain was intense. Terry bent down to try to lift his foot free, but to no avail. The thick, snake-like root tightened around his ankle, slowly crushing the bone. Blood filled his boot. The pain was excruciating. He tried to shout, to scream for help, but nothing came: his throat was still coated with Frieda's toxic leaf dust.

Another root appeared, this one even bigger than the first. Terry's eyes couldn't believe what they were seeing, as this second root wrapped itself around his other foot, slowly squeezing and crushing his other ankle. Jack wasn't proud of what he was doing, but he was running on pure emotion now, and wanted to finish the job. Every last bit of energy from every last one of Jack's cells came together, and in one last violent act, took revenge for Frieda. Voicelessly screaming, Terry felt another pull, this one way more forceful, from a deeper place – and down he went.

***

A few days later, a visibly upset Rob could be seen putting up posters all over the park. Alongside the image of Terry, they read: 'MISSING. Last Thursday, Terry Payne, 39, local tree surgeon, went missing in Clissold Park after felling a large horse chestnut by the Green Lanes entrance. If you have any information on Terry's whereabouts, please call our hotline'.

That night, as dusk fell, Jack contracted his bark, the cells squeezing and pushing together to force out the pins holding the MISSING poster. And Terry's face fell to earth.

MAY

The hunter

His body was positioned at 45 degrees to the ground, head in the soil, bottom in the air, erect tail cutting a series of ever-more-excited circles in the air. No one and nothing was going to stop him.

"Eric!"

Astrid's concerned voice was absorbed by the dense woodland; the beagle continued despite her protestations. An early morning shower had made the ground soft and malleable – perfect conditions for digging.

She leant her stout frame against a nearby tree and let out a quiet sigh. This was the usual. In the park by 10am, Eric would chase the odd squirrel, pee in a puddle while drinking the puddle, and then the main event: smelling and digging, as Astrid waited patiently, thinking of Tony and coffee.

Although today, it did strike her as curious that Eric had returned to the same tree for the third day in a row, attacking the burnt-looking area around the roots of a large oak as if he was having a flashback to his drug sniffing days at Heathrow. Maybe he was about to roll back the years and find a kilo of crack. She somehow doubted it.

Astrid turned towards the ponds and saw Poppy, who no doubt would be very pleased to see Eric. Walking quietly and stoically behind the lively cockapoo was Margaret. It was the first time Astrid had seen her since Keith had died.

"Hi, Margaret," said Astrid respectfully.

"Oh, hi, Astrid. Sorry, didn't see you there," Margaret replied.

"Hiding behind my tree as usual," Astrid said with a thin smile, hoping the joke would ease the conversation, before dutifully following up with, "I'm so sorry about Keith."

Margaret gave a nod and a barely audible, "Yes."

"It must've been such a shock. Do you fancy getting a coffee sometime and having a chat?" continued Astrid. "Maybe at Tony's café?"

"Yes, I'd like that," replied Margaret before she continued on her way, carefully avoiding Eric and his growing pile of soil.

The woodlands were on the north side of the park behind the ponds: a densely populated area of trees and shrubs where the local teenagers smoked weed, did canisters and had sex, probably in that order, thought Astrid. Thankfully she'd never witnessed such events.

For Eric, though, it wasn't a den of iniquity, but rather a haven of odours and discoveries you didn't find in the open spaces of the park. Here he could snuffle away without fear of interruption.

Astrid reached into her damp anorak pocket for the lead. She didn't mind the cold, she'd grown up with that in Norway, but the wet was something she could do without. Not that it bothered her trusty sidekick, whose entire head and chest were now sunk in the ground.

"Eric!"

She waddled over, carefully negotiating the spring growth, but still wincing on every other step.

"This is not helping my hip, young man!"

Eric easily evaded the lead.

"Oh, do come on." She sighed, exasperated, nearly stepping in the mound of excavated earth. A moment later, he reversed out, crumbs of soil glued to his nose and long, elastic strings of spittle hanging from either side of his mouth. In his jaw was something dark and gnarled, which he dropped in front of her like a ceremonial offering.

He barked loudly, head tilted proudly upwards, letting the world (or at least the park) know that his work was done, tail once again whipping the air.

Astrid barely gave the ugly dark root a second glance, gently kicking it with her wellington boot back towards Eric.

"Yes, very good. Now pick it up, whatever it is you're excited about, and let's go."

Eric seemed to get the message when the lead was pulled tight. He picked up his bounty and they trotted off in the drizzle to the café.

***

Tony could set his clock by their visits. They'd been coming in as long as he could remember. Initially, he'd thought they'd be the first of many customers over the years, returning for his home-made pasta and warm hospitality. But it had never turned out like that.

Within three months of opening, he'd had to close the kitchen and let the two waiters go. Instead of serving delicious plates of linguine and glasses of chilled Gavi, he now offered just coffee and snacks, that was all the locals wanted. In his mind, it wasn't really even coffee – not like back home – it was just hot brown milk. Gallons of the stuff.

"Morning, Tony," Astrid offered brightly as she bumbled in, pulling a damp strand of grey hair from her rosy cheek and clipping it behind her ear. She gave Tony her sweetest smile, knowing full well the weather wouldn't have helped his mood.

Tony gave his best 'Tony smile', a weird lip curl showing a bit of teeth, which he thought was charming, but she thought made him look as though he was constipated.

She lifted herself up onto a stool by the window to relieve her hip, but also to show passers-by there was life in Tony's Café and encourage others to follow. No one ever did, but it had become a habit to watch the world go by at an elevated height.

The calm was broken by a high-pitched screeching from the Conti CC100 commercial coffee machine which, like its owner, was not in great shape.

Tony held the small steel jug in place, barely reacting to the cacophonous racket or the droplets of boiling milk splashing onto the back of his hand. He stared vacantly at the map of Italy on the wall, pressing a curly corner back onto the dry Blu Tack.

He glanced over at Astrid, framed in the window, looking sweet and alert, full of life and positivity. *Where does she get it from?* he wondered.

Eric's tail swished across the lino floor as Tony placed the coffee in front of Astrid, ensuring the chipped edge of the saucer was facing the park and the chocolate cappuccino heart was looking up at her.

"Thank you, Tony. How are we today?"

"Amazing," he replied in a deep, dead-pan voice. "Since I saw you yesterday, I have won the lottery, met the woman of my dreams and opened my one hundredth restaurant."

Astrid wanted to reach up and give him a great big hug, but she'd tried that before and it hadn't worked; at five foot and six foot four respectively, it was awkward to say the least.

"How is my furry friend?" Tony reached down to scratch behind Eric's ear. Eric let out a satisfied groan and dropped his discovery on the floor.

"What's this? No stick today?"

Tony bent to inspect the gnarled offering. He wiped the surface and felt the texture, fingers running over the dark, bobbly surface. He took a closer look and got a scent, a pungent smell. He glanced up at Astrid and continued caressing it in his large hands, this time more carefully, bringing it close to his face for a good look, inhaling the intoxicating odour once more.

He couldn't believe it. It wasn't some old root or stick. It was a truffle. One of the largest he'd ever seen. Maybe a Burgundy. It was staggering to see one in London, a piece of black gold filling the palm of his hand.

He glanced at Astrid again and his face suddenly felt different. He was smiling. A real, genuine smile. He held it up and said, "Do you mind if I hold onto this?" Astrid sensed a tiny change in him.

She tucked another strand of hair neatly behind her other ear and proclaimed: "Tony, please keep our dirty stinky root thing. Think of it as a gift from Eric and me to you this Tuesday morning."

***

He shut the café early that afternoon and spent the next hour or so with the truffle. First, he weighed it. Coming in at nearly 400g, it was big. He couldn't quite believe Eric had managed to fit it in his mouth. A quick online search revealed it could be worth over £1700. It was a Burgundy truffle as he'd thought, firm with a little give and very pungent, the *sol de la terre* filling the small kitchen.

He gave it a wipe with a brush and placed it on a chopping board, gently moving it around every few seconds to get a 360° view, as if it were some product demo on a cooking show. Then he carefully put it in an airtight container and stored it safely in the fridge.

He was feeling giddy with excitement. He poured himself a large Campari and soda with loads of ice and, after a rummage around in the kitchen drawer, found himself a Marlboro Red. He took great delight in blowing smoke rings towards the peeling paint on the ceiling like he was sixteen again. He turned the music up – a bit of Miles Davis – the trumpet solo causing the map to vibrate subtly on the wall.

But joy was soon tempered by guilt over what to say to Astrid. Taking the prized jewel from Eric's jaws started to weigh heavy, and he was restless all evening. At 2am he returned to the kitchen and took a shot of Campari from the fridge. As he knocked it back, he spotted a nodule on the surface of the truffle, like an eye watching him through the Tupperware.

Across the park, Astrid was having a different kind of night, an even deeper sleep than normal, comforted by the smile on Tony's face from earlier. She'd even shared her sausages with Eric in celebration and wondered briefly why Tony had been so excited about the root.

But, in a way, she didn't care. If Tony was happy, she was happy.

***

The next morning, Astrid and Eric arrived at the café early. Tony was ready for them, sitting at a table waiting; in front of him was the truffle. He didn't say a word, merely indicating with his hand for Astrid to sit.

And then it all came out. The value of the truffle and how he hadn't slept and how he'd wanted to call her and tell her and how he'd decided after a few phone calls back home he was going to open the café as a restaurant, cooking the truffle just like Mamma used to when they were kids, with the pepper and the fresh pasta and the perfect amount of shaved truffle, all washed down with a glass of Gavi.

She'd never heard him talk so much, so enthused, so passionate. She nodded and smiled and stayed on the chair even though her hip was beginning to ache.

"Well, with all that in mind, I think you're going to like this morning's haul."

Astrid reached into her pocket and produced a handful of dark, root-like objects. She placed them on the table next to the pristine truffle: "Eric got up extra early today."

There was a thud on the floor. Eric adding his final offering. Another truffle. Tony tried to take it all in, whispering quietly many Italian words that Astrid had never heard before. She smiled proudly at Eric. "Who's a clever boy then?"

**

The smells coming from the kitchen were incredible. Eric's inky black nose was on high alert, twitching left and right and up and down. The woodlands had nothing on this. Astrid gently pushed the door, spotting Tony at the stove with his back to her, his large frame partly covered by a small apron.

She cleared her throat and said in a mock serious voice: "Er, excuse me, Mr Tony, table for two please?" Tony turned, wiping his hands on the apron, excitement in his eyes.

"I've got so much to do!" He lifted a wooden spoon from the pan on the stove. "Here... what do you think?"

"I think it's a bit tight, Tony."

He looked down sheepishly at the apron and chuckled.

"It's Mamma's. I found it when I was reading her recipe last night."

Astrid took a taste and her face lit up.

"Yum! Maybe a tiny bit more truffle?"

Tony delicately shaved a couple more slices before stirring them into the sauce. As he continued to cook Astrid got to work on the blackboard:

Truffle Tuesdays @ Tony's Café
From 26th May
6pm–9pm
#TruffleTuesdays

The writing was swirly and fun, and Astrid even managed to draw the logos of Instagram and Twitter. It had all happened within a matter of days. Tony had found his mum's recipe. A few calls back home to check on how best to cook the truffle. "Antonio, bambino, remember the truffle is sensitive – it needs love – warm in butter, not olive oil."

Then Astrid had showed Tony how to get on the social platforms and printed up a few flyers for her friends, who had dropped them into the local shops and houses over the weekend. The stage was set.

***

At first there was only a trickle of diners, one or two locals and friends of Astrid's book group. But the review in the *Islington Gazette* changed everything, calling his pasta 'the greatest truffle pasta this side of Milan'.

Before he knew it, Tony was cooking for a full house every Tuesday and trending on various foodie blogs and Twitter feeds. The most regular customers were the pretty

Turkish girl and her Ed Sheeran lookalike boyfriend, who seemed to enjoy the romantic table by the window. Tony warmed to them and, knowing they were students, gave them a decent discount. Everyone was talking about #TruffleTuesdays. The stoop was gone, the throaty laugh was back, and Tony couldn't stop smiling at his head waitress.

Astrid couldn't quite believe what had happened but, as ever, was going with the flow, enjoying her new Tuesday evening job.

"How's my master truffle hunter today then?" Tony would say to Eric on every visit back to the kitchen. He was *in paradiso*.

***

One evening, a few weeks later, with the restaurant full as usual, Astrid appeared in the kitchen with two half-eaten plates of pasta. "Table 2. They said it's bland and asked if we'd forgotten to put the truffle in."

Tony had been dreading this moment. His success was going to be his downfall. Every new customer and every fresh bowl of pasta meant more truffle was needed. Of which they had less and less. Tony was having to eke out every morsel, using his finest razor blade to slice the precious truffle thinner and thinner. He had even resorted to bulking out the dishes with porcini mushrooms, but that was only going to get them so far, tonight being a case in point.

"Tell them sorry, no need to pay and give them a glass of Gavi on the house."

He wiped the sweat from his forehead and opened the fridge. The cooling air was welcome, as was a little tot of Campari. He could barely look at the Tupperware on the top shelf. He knew it was virtually empty.

He'd already refused several hopeful diners on the phone today, saying the café was full. But if those same people were to walk past this evening, they would see that the place was empty. He took his apron off and threw it in the corner, just missing Eric's head.

He felt annoyed, mostly with himself, for thinking it would work out. The heady excitement of a full restaurant and rave reviews would soon be taken away from him, just when he'd got used to the idea that the place could be a success after all. He'd considered buying in more truffles and had got as far as talking to a wholesaler about the prospect of a regular order. But when he saw the quotes, his heart sank again. To cover the costs, he'd have to nearly double his prices in the restaurant, which he didn't want to do. He gulped the rest of the Campari and had to accept that a truffle-only restaurant was unsustainable.

He turned away from the fridge and saw Astrid out front dealing with the disgruntled customer, nodding, smiling, pouring the complimentary wine and screwing up the bill. She walked back to him with a resigned shrug of her shoulders.

"Thanks," Tony said. "Here." He offered his glass. She took a large swig. Tony rubbed his eyes and looked across at Eric who was sniffing round the fridge.

He watched the curious beagle doing a couple of circuits of the kitchen, his nose no more than an inch off the floor, taking in every imaginable smell. Tony looked at Astrid, eyes alive again.

"I've got an idea."

***

Tony was upstairs in his bedroom, underneath the bed. He shuffled himself out, dusted himself down and shouted. "OK, send him up!"

As he waited a moment, Tony adjusted the Campari poster above his bed so that it was straight, brushing off a bit of dust gathered on the frame. Within seconds, the trusty beagle was in the room, tail wagging, nose skimming the carpet.

"Go for it, Eric. Find it!" Eric raced around the bedroom and, within seconds, came out with a small piece of truffle in his jaws, which he obediently dropped at Tony's feet. "Bravo, my furry friend!"

Tony leant over the banister and held up the morsel of truffle to Astrid like a trophy. Astrid smiled and nodded, but her heart was breaking. What would happen if they couldn't find any more? Since that amazing week finding the truffles, there'd been nothing. It had been an anomaly, she was sure. Maybe they were all gone. After a couple more rounds of hide and seek, Tony was convinced Eric was ready.

"Tomorrow, Astrid, we hunt."

***

Tony stood shivering next to the statue of Lord Clissold, feeling like he too was made of cold metal. He banged his hands together in an effort to get the circulation going. *May. So fickle!* One minute warming sunlight and the promise of an early summer, the next biting wind, sleet and even snow a few weeks back.

He sparked up a cigarette and spotted a small figure waddling along Church Street with a dog on a short lead. He checked in his pocket for the morsel of truffle, which was now beginning to get a bit squishy.

Lloyd unlocked the gates and gave them both a friendly nod as they headed straight for the woodlands. Behind them was another early riser, a demure woman carrying a bunch of flowers, who quickly headed off in the opposite direction.

"Can you remember where?" asked Tony as they approached the woodlands.

"Over there." Astrid indicated a large oak. Tony bent down and held the truffle to Eric's nose, letting him have a good sniff. Eric got to work, racing off into the undergrowth, head low down, nose sweeping the ground.

He scoured the copse, veering left and right like a magnet drawn to an endless cornucopia of smells. Suddenly he stopped and started to dig.

"Go on, Eric!" Tony's voice was full of hope. Astrid had to look away.

Eric dropped a round object at Tony's feet. Tony picked it up and ran his fingers over the surface. It felt too smooth and round, a bit like a tennis ball. Tony scratched the surface to reveal it was a tennis ball. He threw it away.

"No, Eric!" Astrid couldn't bear it as Eric ran off in pursuit of the ball, thinking it was a game.

Tony tried again, encouraging Eric in ever more desperate tones. Eric was a willing soldier, foraging once more, returning time and again with new offerings: a crushed can of K cider, an old shoe, a PFC box, a kid's mitten, but no truffle.

Enough, thought Astrid, who by now had left the woodlands and was resting on Dennis Hickley, 19th August 1919–27th January 2015 'Keen birdwatcher who loved the ponds'. She called out in a resigned tone, "Come on, you two, let's go back."

Eric was a little confused, looking up at Tony with expectant eyes. Tony looked away, reaching inside his jacket for his cigarettes. He sparked up and took a few heavy tugs, before hooking the lead over Eric's head and trudging back to the café.

***

No words were said. Tony merely carried on walking in a slow, resigned manner straight through the café into the kitchen, only stopping at the fridge to reach for the Campari bottle. Astrid could barely look, busying herself with Eric, checking his lead was attached before shouting out, more in hope than anything else, "See you later, Tony?"

She gently shut the café door, half thinking about turning the sign to say 'CLOSED' but knowing that would irritate him. That was Tony's decision. Eric sensed the mood and kept his head down under the darkening sky.

***

Normally, a hearty bowl of soup and a bit of Radio 4 would lift her spirits, but Astrid still felt sad. There had been so much hope and passion in Tony these past weeks. It felt like she'd seen a new man. Everything about him had been transformed, and it had given her a lift too.

She felt bad in a way, having started it all with that stupid gnarly root. Part of her wishing she'd never brought the bloody thing into the café that day. She looked down at Eric, who was lying on the rug with his head on his paws, peering up at her, somehow sensing things weren't right.

She desperately wanted to call Tony or send him a text, but she knew messages would only darken his state of mind. She looked down at Eric before slowly standing up and reaching over to the oven. "There's only one thing for it, Eric – *toscakaka*."

She got down on the floor and swore a little as her hip jarred, before poking her nose into the cupboard for the ingredients for the Scandinavian cake. Eric, sensing things were on the up, sidled up next to her, hoping for some kind of treat or at least a stroke.

***

The 'CLOSED' sign hung at a resigned angle. The shutters were firmly pulled down on all the windows, reflecting the dark skies over Clissold Park. The café looked as if it were about to be repossessed. A young couple walked past and tried the door. They peered in for signs of life and checked their phones. They tried the door one more time before walking off in search of alternative restaurants.

***

Astrid was willing the clock to get to six. At least then she could have a gin and tonic. Things would have to be appalling to start before then. The shortbread was cooked, she'd had three cups of tea and listened to a couple of dull plays on Radio 4. But her patience snapped, and she decided more positive action was needed. She hung the apron on the back of the door and cut two large slices of cake, wrapping them in foil and putting them into a Tupperware.

"Well, like it or loathe it, Mr Tony, we're coming over." And with that, she grabbed Eric's lead and headed out the door.

As she wandered over, she tried to gauge her approach. Uber-positive, maybe shower him with compliments and reassurances and general good vibes? Or go the other way? A bit of cussing, empathy, maybe she should join him in a cigarette? She'd not had one for years, but if it would help, she was up for it. All bets were off, she decided.

Eric scratched at the café door before she even had time to knock. No response. She tapped gently at first, then louder, then had a look in through the window where she thought she could see some flickering light. She tried the phone: nothing.

A large sigh.

"Tony!" she shouted up at his bedroom. She thought about throwing stones, but no. She had pride. She turned away and stomped off towards the park.

"Table for two, madam?"

The deep resonant voice caught her unawares, but wonderfully so. She'd never been so happy to hear that gravelly voice. She turned and couldn't help but break into a smile, even though thirty seconds earlier she'd vowed to give him a piece of her mind instead of a piece of shortbread. Seeing him in his mother's apron was the clincher.

Eric led the way back into the café, which did not look as it had a few hours ago. Tony had clearly been busy. The tables and chairs had all been pushed to the side, leaving just one heroic setting in the middle. Surrounding it were candles, literally hundreds of them all over the café floor, flickering in a small gust of wind as the door closed behind them. On the table were two place settings, a bottle of Gavi in an ice bucket and a framed picture of Eric.

Astrid wasn't a woman for crying, but this nearly pushed her over the edge.

She saved herself with a health and safety gag: "I think you'll find that many candles are a fire hazard, sir," before giggling and melting into Tony's huge, outstretched arms. It was a warm, natural, cosy cuddle which Astrid never wanted to end.

Tony broke off and gestured for her to sit down.

"Two minutes."

"Tony, I'd have got dressed up if I'd known."

But he was gone into the kitchen, Miles Davis turned up a notch, returning with two plates of truffle spaghetti and a bottle of Gavi. He poured the wine, before raising a glass.

"I saved the best until last."

"But I thought it was all gone?"

"Not quite. I figured this moment may come and didn't want to waste the last morsels on a customer, when my head waitress was much more deserving."

***

The next morning, Astrid couldn't stop smiling. From the depths of despair to being serenaded by Tony in the restaurant, drinking Campari until the wee hours and even a small kiss. She nearly tripped over, thinking of it, as Eric led the way into the woodlands. She didn't want to overanalyse it, but just enjoy it for what it was. Eric had headed off and was nowhere to be seen.

"Eric?"

She wandered off into the undergrowth and there he was, tail wagging, not digging this time but just standing in front of a large, darkened patch of foliage. Astrid bent down, cursing her hip a little, but what she saw took her mind off the pain.

"Oh, Eric!"

Wild mushrooms. Hundreds of them stretching out like a blanket of bluebells across the copse, right up to the fence of the flats adjacent to the park. It was an oasis, more than enough to make the odd plate or two of *pasta fungi* and feed the locals once again. She gathered a handful and put them into one of Eric's poo bags before hobbling off in the direction of the café.

***

"There're loads of them, Tony, and there's also fennel and wild garlic. Look!" Astrid held out two handfuls of pungent-smelling leaves. "It's amazing. With my window box of herbs, we could create a proper menu, a forager's feast, and who knows, we could even open more than one day a week? Mushroom pasta, wild garlic risotto, dandelion and nettle soup – that's three dishes right there!"

It all came out in a rush with barely a breath, and she'd hardly touched her coffee, the cappuccino heart looking up at her, crusting a little on the surface. He'd never seen her talk so much, so enthused, so passionate about something. He could feel himself smiling and nodding.

"*Si, bella.*"

He leant forward to give her a kiss, only to be rudely interrupted by a loud bark from under the table. Astrid reached into her pocket and threw Eric a treat. With Eric's back turned, they resumed their embrace.

***

Two weeks later a blackboard appeared outside the café:

Welcome to the Forager's Café
Locally sourced ingredients
Tuesdays & Thursdays
6pm–9pm

JUNE

The Clissold Cowgirl

Abimbola stared into his eyes. Huge brown globes with infinite depth, their gentle power slowly pulling her in. She felt light-headed, floaty, out of control. She could feel herself leaning forward; any minute now their noses would touch. *Does he know how I feel? Does he feel the same? Does he know how important he is?*

A fly landed on his buttock, swished away by his long white tail. A few wisps of straw danced in a shaft of light breaking through the stable door. She stepped back as he adjusted himself, ears twitching, getting settled. The spell was broken. She reached into her hoodie pocket and retrieved two sugar lumps: one each. He crunched through his in no time, long pink tongue licking the palm of her hand and sleeve, checking for leftovers.

"Good boy, Hope," she whispered before eating her own cube. She grabbed the plastic comb and returned to his tangled mane.

"Five minutes, Abi!" a voice shouted from the back of the stables.

She didn't look up, focusing instead on a stubborn knot that was nearly as tight as the one developing in her stomach. Mick was only doing his job; he had to lock up by 9pm. But she hated this last call, knowing their time was over.

Thursday evenings were always a bit of a rush. She'd dump her school bag at home, get changed and grab some toast before getting to the farm by 5pm, patiently waiting for the last visitors to leave before going in.

She always felt a moment of calm walking in, leaving behind home and school and beef with her brother, swapping them for the pungent muddy stables with their noisy inhabitants, unaware and uncaring of the city outside. It was the same routine every week: gallops on the grass, then a few small jumps, before grooming and treats in the stables.

It had been ten years since she'd first laid eyes on him. She always remembered that day. They'd gone on a family trip to the farm. It seemed huge back then, the big entrance gates, the long stables, the bales of hay piled high up to the roof. And, of course, there was the overpowering smell of the animals. Her dad and brother, Deji, were larking around, holding their noses, making juvenile jokes about poo-farts. Mum wasn't impressed and told them both off. Abi took it way more seriously. The smell was just another part of the overall experience which she loved. It felt like another world, and at the heart of it was a little white horse. Seeing the fragile foal taking his first steps had unearthed something deep and maternal inside her. This feeling had grown stronger over the years, reinforced when she became a farm volunteer just after her twelfth birthday. For the past four years, she'd done Thursday evenings after school and most Sundays. Hope now towered over her at eighteen hands and nearly three quarters of a tonne in weight. But he was still her boy.

She finished brushing his hind legs, the warm brown skin of her hand drawing long, arcing strokes over his white coat. His upper lip quivered in appreciation.

The naked light bulb hanging from the wooden rafter momentarily flicked on and off. It was Mick's signal that time was up. You didn't mess with Mick. He'd go on for days if you didn't leave on time. Abimbola stood back for a minute and admired her handiwork. "Who's a handsome boy then?" before returning the stool to the corner of the pen and hanging up the brush. She stroked his velvet-soft nose.

"Be good. See you Sunday." The huge brown eyes blinked and watched her all the way to the gate. She zipped up her hoodie.

"Night, Mick!" she shouted into the darkness.

"Night, Abi!" the darkness replied.

She exited past the 'Welcome to Cally City Farm' sign onto Sheringham Road, hands deep in pockets, walking home to God-knows-what madness. She smelled her cuff and smiled. Only three days…

***

"Oh my God you *stink*."

"Shut up, Deji. Leave me alone." Abimbola tried to force her way past her older brother, but he stood firm.

"Seriously do you ever wash? Skank."

"Mum! Tell him!"

All the good work of the previous three hours undone before she'd even got in the door. They were on a bad run. Teenagers living at close quarters with hormones off the scale. Mum and Dad did their best, but it was a constant battle.

Things had got worse since Deji's moped had been stolen. He'd saved for months, not going out or buying any clothes, just keeping his head down working, getting as many shifts as KFC could offer. Abimbola had been so angry for him. What right did people think they had, taking what wasn't theirs, coming along in the middle of the night, stealing from under their noses, threatening them with a claw hammer?

"Deji, enough," said Mum coming out of the kitchen, playing peacemaker as usual. "You'll wake your father." Dad had recently started working nights, which made living together even harder. "Abimbola, get in there. There's water in the sink. Clean up. Deji, dinner in five minutes."

Mum helped Abimbola out of her hoodie before throwing it in the washing basket.

Abimbola washed her hands before sitting quietly at the kitchen table, stomach rumbling at the delicious smells coming from the large pot on the stove. She spotted an opened letter by her mum's plate. Although it was upside down, she recognised the farm's logo. Intrigued, she reached over and started to read. After a few sentences, she wished she hadn't.

'Due to funding cutbacks, Cally City Farm will need to close for the foreseeable future. We will retain a skeleton staff to care for the animals for the next few months. After next weekend, volunteers will not be required'.

Mum returned to the kitchen but stopped in her tracks when she saw the deflated figure at the table. Abimbola glanced up and they held each other's gaze, before two shiny rivers trickled down Abimbola's hot cheeks, landing salty on her lips.

"I know," said Mum gently. "It only came this morning. There was an email too. We'll think of something. Don't worry, love. It'll be OK, I promise."

Deji was stood in the doorway behind Abimbola and rolled his eyes, but for once didn't say anything.

***

The days that followed were surreal; Abimbola felt her whole world had collapsed. She was lethargic and irritable, spending hours on the balcony, staring blankly across the expanse of Clissold Park, ignoring all phone calls and messages.

Mum braided her hair which helped, but her thoughts soon swung back to Hope and the ache in her stomach returned.

She called Mick in the vain hope he'd somehow say it was all a mistake and they'd be back to normal at the weekend. But no, it was true: Mick was more upset than she'd ever known. She thought he'd been crying, but he claimed he just had a bit of a cold. However, he persuaded Abi to help Janet out with the reindeer in the park. He thought it would take her mind off Hope, even if it was just for a day or two.

Initially Abi couldn't face it, but it turned out to be exactly what she needed. Janet got her involved with feeding the herd, Blitzen immediately taking a shine to Abi, or rather her hoodie, nuzzling keenly at the lingering smell of Hope on the cuffs. As they wandered around the pen, Janet told Abi how she'd met Mick years ago when they were buying animal feed from the same wholesalers. And then bumped into him at the Highbury Barn pub on quiz nights.

Abi spotted a glint in Janet's eye as she talked about Mick, caressing her pearl earring in nostalgic fashion. And, for a moment, Abi saw Janet in a different light. Cool green eyes framed by delicate wisps of white hair and the hint of a cheeky smile. *She must've been a bit of a stunner when she was younger*, thought Abi.

"You and Mick were having a thing!" exclaimed Abi in a loud, spontaneous outburst, nudging Janet in the ribs.

"Shh, Abi, stop that," replied Janet. "We're just good friends." But her previously pale cheeks flushed, telling a different story.

Still, after a couple of fun weeks together it was clear there wasn't enough work for the two of them, so with a leaden heart, Abi gave Janet a big hug, promised to stay in touch and headed back home.

The next day she was back on her bed, staring at pictures she'd posted of Hope on Instagram, enlarging the images with her fingers, feeling his loneliness more than ever. She tugged at her nose ring – her anxiety tic – twisting and gently pulling, satisfying low levels of pain to try and distract from the thought of her boy holed up like a prisoner in solitary confinement.

Enough was enough. She jumped off the bed, grabbed her bag and slipped out of the house, silently pulling the front door shut, trusty sugar lumps and a pair of pliers from Dad's toolbox in her pocket.

***

She knew there was a small hole in the back fence. She worked it with the pliers until it was just big enough to get her slim body through. She used her phone torch to navigate in the dark, but still stumbled on one of the jumps, cussing as she fell to the ground. But with her face in the dirt, she managed a grin; her nostrils had picked up the smell, and she was moments away from being with him again. As she reached the stable door, she heard footsteps behind her and froze. A beam of light hit the back of her head.

"Oi! Stay right where you are. You're trespassing. I'm calling the police."

That voice couldn't belong to anyone else. She turned round. "Mick, it's me, Abi."

"Abi, my God, you nearly gave me a heart attack. What on earth?"

"Sorry, I couldn't help myself."

He sighed. "It's OK. Let's go inside."

They made their way in and sat on a couple of upturned buckets. A few tears were shed. Mick reached into his jacket pocket and retrieved a small flask of whisky, offering Abi a sip, which she politely declined. After a sizeable swig for himself, which he managed while still keeping his half-smoked rollie in the corner of his mouth,

Mick handed her a set of keys. He cleared his throat and spoke quietly.

"Not a word."

Abimbola's face lit up.

"You serious? But what…"

Mick held his finger to his lips.

"It's my spare set. The animals love you, Abi, especially Hope. I've never known anyone care for a horse so well. We can take it in turns."

Abimbola felt a tinge of pride, which turned into a smile that spread across her face. Mick was a sucker for it, especially when the dimples kicked in.

"You're a good girl, Abimbola." Mick was in full flow and Abi knew not to interrupt. She looked into his bloodshot, tired eyes as he continued with his emotive speech, gently twisting the gypsy ring on his tobacco-stained forefinger. "The world needs more Abimbolas. You have something special about you, girl, I've never seen before."

She smiled, wishing she could tell Mick how much he meant to her. He gave her a wink and headed off, attempting to relight his rollie as he went out the stable door.

There were still tears in her eyes as she stroked Hope's nose and sank into the warm cocoon of his mane. She could stay here forever. She wiped away the tears and wondered what she'd do without Mick. She looked at Hope with new purpose in her eyes.

"OK, it's just me and you now, Hope. You ready for this?"

She realised this was the chance she'd been waiting for all these years: to have Hope to herself, at least until the farm returned to normal.

Before she could change her mind, she grabbed Hope's brushes and cloths and some feed before saddling up. Her heart was pounding. With both hands, she gathered her braids and tied them under her riding hat. She zipped up her hoodie and mounted Hope. The clop of the hooves on the hard concrete pathway roused a dusty pig, who let out a snort which Abimbola took as a seal of approval.

"Don't worry, we'll be back before you know it."

The once-distant hum of the city was now fully in Hope's ears, which turned this way and that, taking in the novel sounds. Abimbola guided him past a street light onto the road. She leant down and whispered in his ear, "Listen, we're going to be OK. Just do what I tell you."

***

Ali had seen many things over his years running the Arsenal Mini Market on Blackstock Road: riots, car accidents, drug busts and even the odd celebrity. But Abimbola from the flats riding a huge white horse up to the shop window was a new one. The horse was enormous, but for all the size of the beast, he noted it was calm and she seemed to have it under control, which was impressive.

He continued to stare as she dismounted in one neat movement, diligently attaching the horse's reins to the bike stand. She gave the knot a final pull, before walking into the shop. Ali put his worry beads down and proclaimed: "Aye aye, who do you think you are? The Lone Ranger?"

Abimbola smiled politely. She loved Ali. He was large and solid, like an uncle to her. She didn't always get his jokes, which seemed to be from another time, but in a way, that just added to their relationship.

"All right, Ali. What's up?"

Ali realised she was way too young to get the gag. The Lone Ranger? What was he thinking? Undeterred, he tried again.

"The horse? What's all that about?"

"Long story," replied Abimbola.

"Well, I'm not going anywhere, young lady. Try me. I'm all ears."

She picked up a bunch of overly ripe bananas and plonked them on the counter, holding out her money. He pushed it away.

"Nah, you have them. They've virtually gone off, to be honest. I presume they're for the big fella?"

"His name is Hope," she said in a mock tough-guy accent.

"Oooo…" Ali loved the chat. "Well, I 'hope' to see you both again soon."

She breezed out and fed Hope a banana which he gulped down whole. Adjusting her Nike high-tops in the silver stirrups, she leant sideways just far enough to see Ali. He gave her a cowboy finger-gun gesture which was reciprocated by Abi's playful middle finger, before she pulled the reins and told Hope to 'giddy up'.

***

After the breakfast bananas, they clip-clopped slowly and majestically down the centre of Riversdale Road, a couple of new faces in town to brighten the days of the working-from-homers, if only they cared to look up from their screens.

At first, Clissold Park seemed not to impress Hope, who stood motionless just inside the gate, rubbing himself on the statue of Lord Clissold, ignoring Abimbola's encouraging little kicks. His head was slightly raised, nostrils flaring at a smorgasbord of new smells. He took in the vista – over fifty-five acres of one of London's larger parks – which suddenly brought on the desire to run. Not a canter or gentle stroll, but an intense gallop across the park that a thoroughbred half his age would be proud of.

He narrowly missed a personal trainer and a few surprised dogs, but didn't put the brakes on in time to stop himself from landing in the New River, tossing Abimbola over the top into the shallow, murky water. She was soaked. She adjusted her riding hat, which had stayed on, and peered up to see the personal trainer with a look of astonishment on his face.

"Sorry! He's never done that before, I swear," she apologised.

Abimbola couldn't quite believe it. She'd thought a nice gentle stroll in Clissold Park would get Hope used to this new world, but clearly, he had other things on his mind. As she caught her breath, she heard a passing mum mutter, "That's disgusting." She looked down and saw Hope had left a stinking brown pile slap bang in the middle of the walkway, which no buggy, mum or jogger could easily avoid. The smell hit Abimbola's nostrils and, for once, wasn't welcome.

In the nearby park-keeper's shed, Lloyd was taking his first sip of tea and whispered under his breath, "What the…?" at the sight of horse and rider in the stream. He hoped Rob hadn't seen, otherwise there'd be trouble. Lloyd headed out to have a quiet word.

"You OK?"

Lloyd thought he'd keep it casual to start.

"Yeah fine, bit wet," replied a massively embarrassed Abimbola.

He pushed a rogue dreadlock back under the side of his hat, eyes squinting in the morning sun, remembering he'd left his shades in the buggy.

"You're from the flats, aren't you?"

Abimbola nodded. He knew she was a good kid, but he still had his job to do.

"I know your brother Deji, right? Works at the KFC on Upper Street?"

Abi nodded.

"Had his moped stolen the other day?"

She nodded again and nearly started in on the moped gang and how she hated them and how they'd sort of ruined Deji's life. But she thought better of it and kept quiet.

"You know you're not really supposed to be in here with, erm, a horse," said Lloyd. When it was said out loud, Abimbola realised it sounded ridiculous. But she remained silent, biting the inside of her lip. Lloyd continued.

"You see, the rules state that the only animals allowed are dogs. We've never had horses before, maybe a couple of hundred years ago when Lord Clissold was cruising his estate, but not now. Don't get me wrong, I'd say you're OK, but Rob, the guy I work with, he's a real stickler. So, just wanted to warn you."

84

Abimbola nodded, grabbed Hope's reins and squelched off, painting dark, wet footprints on the pathway as she went.

Lloyd gave her a little salute. "Take care, Clissold Cowgirl."

***

After the inauspicious start, Abi was cautious, not just about the possibility of Hope running into someone, but also the fact the park-keepers, Lloyd and Rob, could eject her at any moment. She talked it through with Mick back at the farm, who had a few tips. "Always carry sugar lumps and a carrot. You never know when you're going to need them. Don't forget, Hope will be a bit nervous when you take him out of his comfort zone. And I'd say, time your run into the park when Lloyd is on. I know him from a while back, nice bloke, more relaxed than that Rob, who's a bit of a fusspot."

Mick leant forward and relit his rollie before taking a large drag and exhaling, the smell of rolling tobacco filling the air between them. Abi would never admit it, but it was a smell she loved.

"Thanks, Mick."

Wise words indeed. Lloyd seemed to like her and even welcomed Hope's stinking brown piles, which were the perfect compost for his beloved rose garden in front of Clissold House. Rob was more the issue, so she'd taken to using the hill behind the tennis courts first thing in the morning as a viewing post. Against the intense endless blue sky, she'd sit on the back of Hope in retro denim shorts, white T-shirt and shades, like a modern-day desperado, keen brown eyes hidden behind her aviator sunglasses, scouring the landscape below for fussy park-keepers.

Abi was happiest when Lloyd was on shift. She'd got used to his movements and knew his schedule off by heart. Their relationship had developed so much that Lloyd would sometimes look after Hope. But it was at a price. At the end of the week, Abi would have to pay Lloyd back for the animal care with a large takeout. Lloyd had christened it 'Friday Feast-Day'.

"OK, Lloyd. What'll it be?" asked Abi.

"Need you ask?!" Lloyd replied.

***

They were in heaven, thanks to Bling Wings the new chicken joint on Highbury Park. They carefully spread the food cartons on Yvette O'Keefe, 1940–2012 'Happy memories in this park', before tucking in, relishing the tangy buffalo sauce and double-fried chips. Lloyd rated it highly. It was way better than PFC but probably not quite as good as KFC, which just edged it, thanks to the friendly insults from Deji.

The evening sunshine warmed Abimbola's skin and she wasn't sure if life got any better than this.

The moment was broken by a familiar sound: the roar of mopeds being ridden across the park by the gang who'd taken to terrorising the locals. Rob and Lloyd were united in their hatred of the moped gang, but could never catch them. They were way too fast for the electric park buggy and every time the police were called, they'd arrive too late. This summer had been the worst and Rob was champing at the bit to catch them.

One of them raced past, pulling a wheelie with one hand and giving Abi and Lloyd the finger with the other. The second rider did the same, this time much closer. As he rode past, Abi froze. She'd spotted the 'DJ' tag on the back of the scooter's seat.

"Oh my God, that's Deji's moped!" She drew her hand up to her face, taking her shades off to get a better look, her eyes virtually bursting out of their sockets: "That's the bastard who nicked it!" Abi didn't even think about it; she threw her food down and ran to Hope.

Lloyd shouted through a mouthful of chicken, "Abi! No, wait!" But it was too late. She was up and off in a flash.

The mopeds roared away. The drivers looked at each other, laughing like hyenas as they sped under the canopy of trees towards the ponds. They swerved to avoid a busy beagle crossing their path, ending up in the woodlands where they struggled, not just with the terrain but also the low-lying branches causing them to duck and lose balance. Abi weaved effortlessly through the foliage; she and Hope were on home ground.

One of the mopeds lost control, skidded and smacked into a large oak; the rider was thrown off into the undergrowth, a muffled expletive screamed into the helmet. This brought a satisfied look to Abi's face, but he wasn't the one she wanted. The one on her brother's moped was getting away.

It was a straight run all the way past the willow trees up to the tennis courts. The open pathway favoured the moped again, but with foliage stuck around the front wheel, he was slowing down. Abi was urging Hope on with every stride, shouting in his ears to keep going, heels kicking his flanks, hands gripping the reins tightly.

Some lads from the skate park had seen what was going on and as the moped approached, they put their bikes and boards on the pathway, creating a barricade. The moped skidded and the driver fell off. He dusted himself down, reached inside his jacket and brandished a large claw hammer. He got back on and raced down the narrow pathway towards the cemetery exit and escape onto Church Street.

But Lloyd had driven the buggy all the way round the outside of the park and blocked his path. The rider turned back to see Abimbola and Hope not 20 feet away, staring defiantly at him. Abimbola tightened her grip on the reins. The driver's dark eyes were twitchy, looking around, desperately hoping for a way out, his accomplice and cocksure attitude now long gone.

The evening sunlight glinted off Abi's shades, which momentarily dazzled the rider, causing him to blink and look away. It was all the encouragement Abi and Hope needed, and they raced straight at him. The driver had only one option left – into the small cemetery. But the tightly packed gravestones meant he had no real chance to gather speed, and Hope easily cornered him, leaping majestically over Caroline Hutt 1923–2018, blocking his path and giving him no way out. He threw the moped down onto the side of John Miskin 1919–2015 and slipped through a gap in the fence, but like Lloyd, Rob had followed the action across the park and wrestled him to the ground.

It was over. The goodies had got the baddies. Deji would get his scooter back and from this day forth, Rob would grant Abimbola and Hope the freedom of the park.

The heroine and her mount looked shattered. Lloyd wandered over, patted Hope as steam rose off his warm, sweaty coat, and looked up at Abi.

"What?" Abi said, with a smile and a couple of dimples.

"You did it, girl. You got him," Lloyd said proudly.

Abi pulled the reins and adjusted her sunglasses as if she were indeed the Lone Ranger. "Just doing my job, sir."

And with that, the Clissold Cowgirl and her trusty steed sauntered across the under-elevens' football pitch into the sunset, munching on a couple of well-deserved sugar lumps.

JULY

The mound

The fan was useless. Sitting on a chair beside the bed, just inches from Ali's nose, it whirred in its pre-programmed arcing movements, failing to cool any part of his large, round face, merely recycling warm air from one side of the small suburban bedroom to the other.

He'd tried everything. Cold showers, flannels, drinks. And yet his body still felt like a small furnace.

One of his customers, Janet the park vet, had told him a frozen hot water bottle could help. If you fill one with cold water, freeze it and place in the bed at night, it cools the sheets, aiding peaceful sleep. Apparently, the body needs to be at least one degree cooler than the surrounding air to get to sleep.

Maybe try that tonight, he thought.

He reached out and clicked the fan off, the incessant whirring dying down to silence before the gentle drone of traffic on Green Lanes took over. He checked his phone: 5.30am. His wife stirred next to him, before turning away, settling her head on the pillow. He gently rolled off the bed, grabbed his worry beads and went downstairs. So far this year, temperatures of 38°C and 39°C had been recorded in London. It was now officially the second hottest summer on record. And it was only July.

A shard of light cut across the lino floor, warming his toes. He stared into the fridge, tired brown eyes surveying what was on offer, weighing up the yoghurt or the watermelon. He reached past both for the can of Coke which he slowly and deliberately rolled across his forehead, the cold, metallic surface cooling his warm skin. Like a fan, only better. Plus, you could drink it, which he did, in three greedy gulps.

He was hoping for some respite today, but it seemed to be getting worse. The radio was predicting 40°C by the end of the week. At least the early start meant he could get to the shop before the deliveries. He pulled a fresh T-shirt from the pile of washing on the table and headed out, ensuring all curtains remained firmly closed for the day to try and keep the place cool.

Fat chance.

***

He had a sweat on even though he'd only been walking for a matter of minutes. Sunlight reflected harshly from a passing car's windscreen. *This would be nothing back home,* he thought. Some days it got up to 45°C but somehow you didn't feel it. Life was different on the farm. "This is real work," his dad would say. "Not opening and closing a till, reaching behind for a pack of cigarettes."

At the end of the working day, they would always eat together as a family, a delicious bowl of *imam bayildi*. No microwave meals or takeaways in front of the TV. Good solid home cooking. Ali would be asleep before his head hit the pillow. He'd lose a bit of weight, eat well, feel good about life, even get a bit of a tan.

But if he was honest with himself, after six weeks he'd start to miss the family's other business, the Arsenal Mini Market on Blackstock Road. He knew the lifestyle wasn't good for him, but he just felt more at home on his rickety wooden throne, offering advice and avocados to the people – his people – of N5. He'd been doing it for over twenty years and felt he had a stronger presence here than in the fields of Fethiye in Turkey. He was needed here. Plus, there was better Wi-Fi.

***

Most days, he'd enter the park through the gate on Queen Elizabeth Drive and head round the ponds. If the gates were locked, he'd go through the hole in the fence by the tennis courts.

It all depended on if the park-keepers had opened up. And how Ali was feeling. And today he wasn't feeling his usual ebullient self. It wasn't just the heat or lack of sleep. Energy bills were on the up, shop takings were down, the large drinks fridge was on the blink, and he suspected his daughter, Essen, was still seeing that waste-of-space Josh, when she should be studying.

He crouched down, trying not to scratch his bald head on the fence, but in so doing, forgot the side wires which clawed a small tear in his shirt.

"*Allah kahretsin,*" he cursed in his mother tongue before extracting himself from the fence's wiry grip, emerging into the park. He went past the tennis courts towards the under-elevens' pitch.

That's when he saw it.

And in an instant, he forgot every thought he'd had that morning.

***

At a distance, he thought the sunlight was playing tricks with his eyes. He wiped the sweat from his brow. But there it was. An enormous mound in the middle of the under-elevens' football pitch. It must've been over 200 feet long, stretching from one penalty spot to the other. And at least 30 feet high.

As he got closer, he could see it rose gently from the ground in a natural fashion. He'd never seen anything like it. His eyes blinked wide open, awestruck, trying to take in the sheer scale of the thing. He turned around instinctively, checking if anybody else was there.

It was vast but had a serene presence, like it had always been there, part of the landscape. There was nothing to show it had been put there by some alien force. It felt more like it had come from below, from the earth, rising up.

He got his phone out and held it up to take a picture; he clicked a few shots off, but no angle could fit the whole thing in. He stood back a few feet, but even then, it seemed too big. He returned his phone to the pocket of his jeans and let his eyes do the work. It was an incredible sight that he'd tell his customers about later on. Or rather they'd be telling him, a series of hourly updates no doubt.

The shadows of the trees that normally stretched across the flat, grassy landscape climbed up the slanting sides of the mound, towards the apex. As he stood next to the edge, he could appreciate its size, taking in the scale of it. It was like something from a movie. *Close Encounters* of the Monday morning kind.

He was tempted to climb to the top, but something stopped him. It was like a force field around it made him stay at the bottom. For once, Ali cut a diminutive figure, dwarfed by the enormity of the mound. As he wandered out of the park, he turned for one last look and spotted a fox cautiously walking around its base, tail between its legs.

***

The wooden pallet of fruit and veg was stacked high against the metal shutter of the Arsenal Mini Market. A long receipt on top fluttered in a gust from a passing bus. *That's strange. I thought I was early today.* Ali checked his watch. It had stopped. He let out another quiet expletive and snatched the receipt before raising the steel shutter.

Ali liked his morning routine. Get to the shop in good time, sort the deliveries and then enjoy a moment of calm before the waifs and strays drifted in, getting their essentials and five mins of chat. The bread, beer and loo roll all had to be paid for, but the therapy was free. His surgery, open seven days a week. He couldn't help himself. The shop was an open-plan confessional, where nothing was off limits: jobs, husbands, wives, boyfriends, girlfriends, ex-boyfriends, ex-girlfriends, Arsenal, medical issues – "You ever had a hernia, Ali?" – cars, bikes, mopeds, moped gangs, leaking roofs, exams – "You ever go to college, Ali?" – flatmates, booze, drugs and more Arsenal – "You rate Arteta, Ali?"

Every age, race, sex and colour wanted a bit of one-to-one time. He never judged them. Not even when they'd clearly outstayed their welcome and were blocking the shop and losing him custom. Because one day it could be him on the other side. Life is fragile and you never know when it's going to take you down.

He would always give his trademark smile and a *bon mot* to send them on their way: "You'll be all right, mate", "Tomorrow's another day", "Yep, Arteta's a good man", "Here, have a Kinder Egg. That'll sort it".

The king of the small talk.

However, his mood changed when it came to laying out the veg, thoughts returning to earlier in the year when Josh had been coming into the shop. Ali had unwittingly taken the young lad under his wing, helping in his quest to win the heart of a local girl they'd both named 'Juliet' to Josh's 'Romeo'.

But 'Juliet' had turned out to be Ali's daughter, Essen. And Josh had turned out to be a member of the local moped gang terrorising the locals. Ever since that day when Essen had awkwardly introduced them in the front room, Ali had taken against Josh. No one who was part of a gang was welcome in his home. Essen claimed Josh had changed and had left the gang, but Ali didn't believe her and reluctantly she had agreed to stop seeing him.

The onions and aubergines were a daily reminder of the meal Ali had helped Josh cook to woo Essen. He felt a little sick at the thought of it and looked away, trying to think of something else.

The papers, he decided. *I'll sort the papers.*

He got to work sliding in the supplements, making sure he stashed a spare copy of *The Guardian* and *The Sun* behind the till for himself. He liked to have a broad perspective of the political landscape. He placed the bendy ice-cream sign out front and pastries in the oven out back. And finally, his moment on the stool: black coffee, worry beads and a read. Although today he sensed the news wouldn't be from the papers... but from the park.

***

"Did you see it?" Kenroy the cabbie – a tall, proud Jamaican not shy of giving his opinions on the events of the day – was stood somewhere between the veg, the spice rack and the fridge in his bright-red Arsenal top, pulled taut across his wide chest. He was one of the regulars. Ali liked him. And since he'd been diagnosed with diabetes and prostate problems, Kenroy was a changed man. No more pies and pints, now it was all cardio and tomatoes. Every morning up at 6am Kenroy would power walk 5k around Clissold Park to get himself fit and manage his condition. Ali could learn a thing or two from Kenroy.

"What utter bullshit that was yesterday. Never offside.

My nan could've seen that. And she's blind!" They both roared with laughter. *So here it comes*, thought Ali. *The Arsenal chat.* He'd completely forgotten the result from the day before.

Kenroy, professional football fan, was telling Ali and the spice rack why the Gooners were robbed. Ali was tempted to mention it was only a pre-season friendly, but he'd learnt never to interrupt Kenroy mid-flow. Ali waited for him to finish before asking a non-Arsenal-related question.

"Not in the park then today, Ken?"

"Not today, mate. Celebrating with a lie-in. Blood pressure results came back – all still low."

"Nice one. You take care, bud. Here, catch. This one's for the prostate."

Kenroy caught the complimentary tomato and was gone, leaving Ali to the sports pages, seeing if the journalists agreed with Kenroy's report.

***

"It looks like normal grass, Ali, but when you walk on it it's completely different. It's soft and spongey underfoot, like that stuff they put in playgrounds. So weird."

The first mound report came from Mick the janitor from Cally City Farm. Or at least he thought it was Mick. Ali hadn't seen his face this animated for years. The creases round his mouth filled out into a wide grin. His skin had a glow, and the eyes – normally watery and bloodshot – seemed to have had a mini makeover. Although his smoker's cough still announced his arrival.

"Honestly, it was like I was bouncing on my way over here today."

"Right, gotcha," replied Ali, reaching behind to get Mick his Golden Virginia.

"I was bloody knackered by the time I got to the top, but it's worth it, Ali – it's amazing – you get an incredible view. I could see the roof of the farm from up there."

"Right, gotcha," replied Ali again, handing over the tobacco, hoping Mick hadn't noticed the repeated phrase.

No chance. Mick was that excited he nearly forgot his change.

***

"Lloyd, my man. What's up?" Ali greeted the park-keeper with the usual fist bump across the counter. Lloyd smiled but said nothing, instead reaching into his cargo trouser pocket to retrieve his phone.

"This is what's up."

Lloyd held the slightly battered Nokia up to Ali and played a short video clip of children playing in the park. Ali looked a little bemused.

"And?"

Lloyd played it again.

"Watch the way they're rolling, Ali."

Ali leaned forward on the counter which groaned quietly, and he saw it. Kids rolling *up* the slope of the mound, with no effort, defying gravity and logic, literally rolling up a hill.

"I was there. It's amazing, mate. One of the mums just posted it on Facebook. Never seen anything like it."

Ali looked at the screen and then back at Lloyd. "For real? You sure it's not playing backwards or anything?"

"For real."

The footage ended with the parents laughing and whooping. A mum off-camera is heard to say, "This is so weird." Lloyd returned his phone to his pocket.

"Small bottle of rum please, Ali."

***

And on it went. The day was dominated by reports of the mound. It was like the war in Ukraine, the energy crisis, the heatwave and Arsenal's disallowed goal had never happened.

There was time for one more visitor before Ali finished his shift. Edith. She appeared at the door in her inimitable pose, completely still, holding onto the shop's door frame with one hand and her walking stick in the other, both aiding balance. The only movement came from her eyes, furtively surveying the scene, computing how she was going to get down the short entrance slope, past the papers and up to Ali's counter without keeling over.

She waited for a moment to gather courage and make sure Ali had spotted her. It was only a matter of yards, but when you've had two knee replacements, it was quite a journey, which always needed a little encouragement.

"Here she is, my queen! How you doing, Edith?" Ali was beaming at her.

Edith adjusted her Benny Hill-style glasses, held together on the bridge of her nose with a scruffy piece of masking tape. Her furtive mouse-like eyes behind the crooked spectacles locked on Ali's face, trusting him to guide her in.

"There's no time for that today, young Ali. We need to talk." The voice was slightly posh, stern. Ali loved it.

He rearranged the smile on his face to form a more considered, empathetic look.

"So, what we talking about, Edith?" he asked softly, leaning gently on his counter.

She finally arrived, relief on her face, reaching over the chocolate bars to grip his counter and announce in a loud whisper: "That thing in the park, Ali. That's what we're talking about. What on earth?" A pause. Then a request, "And do you have any croissants left?"

***

Ali listened to her like he had all the others, nodding, smiling, taking their money. It had been constant all day. And now he was very pleased to be handing over to his brother, Yucel, for the evening shift.

"All OK?" Yucel asked. Ali didn't have the energy.

"Yeah, same old, nothing new. Can you call the engineer again? Fridge still dead."

***

The early evening heat was strong. Dogs were still panting; backs of necks were still burning and benches in the shade were still by far the most popular. Ali followed his elongated shadow up the pathway to the fountain. As he stooped down for a sip of water he spotted some fresh graffiti, a clumsily drawn love heart scratched into the stone, together with the letters 'J' and 'E'. He tried not to let his brain race, but it did. *Josh and Essen.* Were they still meeting in secret? Was it going on behind his back, maybe still in the park? His head was throbbing.

He threw some of the water over his scalp and sat on Floyd Williams, 5th February 1998–19th June 2020 'It's not the years in your life, it's the life in your years', thinking what a day it had been: the mound dominating the landscape, kids rolling up it, teens talking selfies in front of it, a busy beagle stubbornly remaining at the bottom barking. *No doubt it won't be long before the local media arrive*, he thought.

***

"Dad, have you seen it?" Essen threw the question at him before he'd even had time to sit down.

"Yes, I have seen it. No, I've no idea. Can you pass me the remote please?"

"Keep your hair on."

They gave each other a knowing smile as she passed the device.

He settled into the dark leather sofa, reaching down to take his shoes off. "Where's your mother?"

"She's gone to Zumba," replied Essen, turning towards the mirror.

"She's left you a salad and a smoothie in the fridge."

"You off out?" Ali asked. No response. The full-length mirror had her complete attention as she went for the pout, glossed lips bunched up, blowing herself a kiss.

"Shouldn't you be studying?"

"Dad! It's fine. Stop nagging."

"Well, before you go, can you do me a favour? Can you get me a hot water bottle?"

Essen stopped looking at herself for a moment and turned to her father, staring directly at him.

"You OK, Dad?"

***

As soon as Rob saw the mound he swung into action and fired off an email to the local councillor, asking if he could visit the park and see if any investigations were needed.

Rob also decided to take action himself and nipped over to Ali's shop and bought fifteen rolls of hazard tape, which he used to cordon off the mound as if a serious incident had occurred overnight.

But it didn't last long, maybe half a day at most, before people were ducking under the black-and-yellow tape or, worse, ripping it apart. There was no way of policing who could and couldn't mount the mound.

Janet, the park vet, and Lloyd had told Rob he was being a killjoy. They tried to explain to him that no one could legally be prevented from walking on a mound in a public park, which, when Rob thought about it, sounded like it might be true. And so he relented.

Ever since the mound had appeared, it was as if the whole community was on a bit of a high. A legal 30-foot high that showed no signs of coming down.

The latest news was that a rare species of flower had been discovered. An anonymous woman had left a note on clissoldpark.com, claiming the fluorescent orange plant to be 'a botanical first'. People had started having yoga classes on it, the Mudra blackboard on Church Street proudly proclaiming 'Outdoor yoga. Top of the mound. 7am. Salute the sun from on high!'. The only wary ones were the foxes and dogs. Rob had spotted Eric the beagle most days, cowering at its base. Birds were also suspicious, often swooping down for a closer look, but never actually landing.

The biggest refuser of all was Ali. He still hadn't had any kind of epiphany even though he passed it twice a day. He'd gone up one night to see what all the fuss was about but felt nothing. He'd even tried lying at the bottom of the mound and rolling uphill like the kids, but to no avail.

It was like he'd been sold the dodgy drugs. While everyone else was on the good gear, floating around in a magical bubble, he'd been given the fake stuff, remaining flat as a pancake. But in an effort not to upset his regulars, he kept the banter going, creating a new set of *bons mots*:

"It's a spaceship."

"It's a message from Allah."

"A message from Arteta."

"It's 10G."

"It's fracking."

"It's a stunt for the next series of *Stranger Things*."

***

The next day, Kenroy appeared in his usual spot with news. More mounds overnight: five small new ones had appeared by the fences along Green Lanes.

Jesus Christ, Ali thought, *it's never going to end.* However, within the hour, the new mounds had been revealed as nothing more than piles of fresh mulch to be spread along the running tracks.

***

By the end of the week, a small area at the centre of the mound had been cordoned off with temporary railings and a couple of small white tents. The council had got involved after Rob's email and they'd invited local earth and soil scientists to have a look at the gravity-defying hill, which was now getting talked about in the local press. Rumours were that the BBC were sending down a news crew at the weekend.

The rare orange flowers from the top of the mound and various soil samples were subjected to all manner of tests in the tents, while a man with headphones and a handheld sonar slowly but surely scanned the length and breadth of the mound. There was even a drone flying high in the sky, taking aerial shots of the mound and the park.

Rob was loving it. He hung around the scientists like a strange groupie, desperately wanting to be in on the action. And then, armed with whatever info he could glean, he would hold centre stage outside his and Lloyd's shed, as if he'd been officially appointed park spokesperson, the 'Mound Man', informing Lloyd and whoever was walking past of the latest developments.

But, after a few days, there was nothing conclusive from any of the tests. It seemed the mound hadn't registered anything unusual, and the operation was packed up. The scientists gave a collective shrug of their shoulders, before leaving the locals to enjoy their magic mound.

***

Saturday was normally Ali's favourite day. Customers were jollier at the end of the working week. Takings were always up at weekends. And if it was sunny, which looked like a given for the rest of the summer, they'd do well on BBQ coals and firelighters and drinks.

But this weekend he didn't feel good. The week had been intense, with no real respite from the tsunami of crap he was facing. Essen and Josh, the fridge, the increase in energy bills. At every turn there seemed to be a problem. And, as predicted, the mercury was about to hit 40°C.

As he walked in the cooling shade from the canopy of trees, he felt confused as to how he was going to get through not just the weekend but the rest of summer. If the heat continued and the fridge was out of action, they were going to miss out on thousands of pounds of income from drinks, which were his best mark-up products.

And then he stopped thinking about fridges and money and heatwaves and drink. Because walking towards him was the biggest problem of all.

A tall lanky one with bright-red hair, and in baggy tracksuit bottoms and an oversized black puffer jacket – possibly the only one being worn in the whole of North London. It was Josh, cutting a diagonal route across the park, no doubt on a sneaky visit to Essen.

"*Orospu çocuğu.*"

The swear words were spat out with venom. The 'son

of a bitch' was going to get it. Ali ran directly at Josh, a buffalo bearing down on a defenceless gazelle. Josh took evasive action and ran up the mound away from danger. But Ali, fuelled by weeks of pent-up anger, found a few extra gears. For a big man, he was surprisingly nimble and made it up the mound, where he and Josh faced each other.

Josh didn't move, standing his ground, albeit somewhat nervously: "Ali stop, wait. What is it?" Somewhat taken aback by the teenager's brave stance, Ali paused, gathered his breath and wiped his mouth.

"I'll tell you what it is, mate. I reckon you're still seeing my Essen when I told you both to stop and it's messing with her studies. And it's messing with my head… and it'll be messing with your head in a minute."

Josh held up his hands in a pleading gesture. But Ali leered aggressively into his face, causing Josh to fall backwards. Josh expected the next thing he was going to feel would be fresh air before a thump onto the ground below. But he remained caught at an angle of 45 degrees, frozen like something from *The Matrix*, as if some special power was keeping him there, safe from falling. Ali was the same, frozen in mid-air.

A second later, Josh was released and sprang back into his earlier position, nose to nose with Ali.

They both looked a bit confused, but Josh realised he still had work to do: "I swear I was on my way over to see Essen now to break it off. She'd told me how upset you were and how important her exams are. I'd never do anything to upset her. Or you." The defence sounded plausible. "I'm not in Matt's moped gang no more. I swear

I'm not, honestly. I'm not, Ali. I only did it a couple of times. They were all caught last month after that girl on the big white horse chased them, remember? I'm nothing to do with them no more."

Ali's aggressive stance eased off as the case for the defence continued.

"I was bullied into it. I only ever did two jobs with them and the last was the day you gave me the recipe."

Ali stared at him, not saying a word, sweat dripping down the small of his back. And in a few other places. It was cooling and welcome, and he started to feel a little lighter about everything. But then a spark of irritation.

"Why didn't she tell me? Why didn't *you* tell me?"

"We weren't sure what you'd say. We were scared. You might not believe us and do something mad. Like throw me off the top of this mound."

They both looked around. A wicked smile appeared on Ali's lips.

"Yeah, she's got a point. Although I'm not sure if it'll let me."

Ali felt a little light-headed and sat down. Josh joined him, but a few feet away. The sun was beating down and, from a certain angle, they looked like a pair of early morning yogis saluting the sun. The large, rounded Buddha and his skinny disciple.

Ali picked a few blades of grass and held them up to Josh. "You know, it looks just like normal grass, but underfoot it's like that bouncy stuff in playgrounds."

"I know right. It's insane," Josh replied, somewhat overenthusiastically. The relief in his voice was palpable.

Ali breathed in the fine air and for the first time in

a long time could see light at the end of the tunnel. He could also see the roof of Cally City Farm. Josh got up and offered Ali his hand.

"Think you'll need two of those to get me up, mate."

But he accepted the gesture and a moment later their hands were locked in a firm handshake, Josh trying not to wince.

"You need to ask me if you want to take her out, OK?"

"Of course, Ali. I'm sorry. I honestly never meant any trouble."

"It's OK, I get it. She's special."

They walked down the side of the mound in bouncy fashion, the rhythm of their moon steps energising them as they came down to earth.

"So, can I take her out, Ali?"

Ali rubbed his stubbly chin.

"I'll think about it."

***

He had to admit he felt better. It may have come late, but he'd finally had his mound moment. The chat up there with Josh had lifted a weight off him. The grassy mound had finally helped the human mind.

That morning, the fridge seemed to have decided to have its own epiphany too, fixing itself overnight, welcoming Ali with its lights on, chilling beers, wines, soft drinks, the lot. Ali grabbed a cool can of Coke and rolled it across his forehead.

It turned out to be a bumper weekend. The heat drove record numbers into the shop and sales were up across the board. He went to bed with his frozen hot water bottle, for once looking forward to the morning.

**

That night, the skies over North London cracked into an epic, driving thunderstorm and a flood drenched the capital. It had been on the cards. That kind of heat was not sustainable said the weathermen, who'd warned of the imminent deluge. Ali kept the windows open all night and listened to the bullets of rain pinging off the roofs of parked cars and the torrents of water racing down the road. He didn't care. He was in no-need-for-that-bloody-fan heaven.

**

The next morning, he slipped through the hole in the fence with no rips or scratches and headed off to the mound with a spring in his step. He was going to go up top and take in a huge breath of the sweet air.

But as he strode purposefully across the park, his stomach did a little lurch at what he saw. Or rather what he didn't see.

It was gone. There was nothing there.

The under-elevens' pitch was flat as a pancake, back to being a normal football pitch.

His jaw dropped a little and a "What the f**k?" crept out.

He looked around, but no one was there to share the deflation. He walked across the grass, trying to find any sign or proof of the mound, searching for the rare orange flowers, treading down with intent on to the turf, hoping to get that bouncy feeling back underfoot. But nothing.

It was like it had never happened. Everything was back to normal. He rubbed his already sweating bald pate before leaving the park.

As he headed down Riversdale Road to work, a fox scampered behind him, running confidently across the pitch.

***

Ali didn't have the time to think about the whys and what ifs of this strange phenomenon. He'd soon have his customers on his doorstep. No doubt needing their supplies and in even more need of a chat.

He laid out the veg and sensed something behind him. He turned to see Kenroy through the shop window, panting a little, slightly wide-eyed.

Before he could get the words out, Ali mouthed: "Yeah, I know."

AUGUST

The birthday girl

The map consisted of four pieces of A3 paper neatly sellotaped together to form the layout of an urban park. It dominated the wall in her small galley kitchen, overlapping a window on one side and slightly folded in on itself against the cupboard on the other.

Like most mornings, Lizzy sat at the table facing the map, studying it as she enjoyed her tea and toast. Today she noticed for the first time that the two ponds on the north side appeared like a pair of wonky, Picasso-esque eyes, looking down over the rest of the park. She liked that, the thought of someone else watching over the place.

A ladybird began to make its way through the reindeer pen, across the children's playground, in a straight line to the tennis courts where it stopped on court eight. It must've come in with the flowers that she bought yesterday. The poignancy of the direction of travel was not lost on her.

The map was pretty much like any other – toilets, café, playground, tennis courts – all clearly marked, except on this one there was the addition of nearly one hundred red and green pins dotted all over the pathways with names and dates on tags, like an incident board from a TV police drama.

She brushed some toast crumbs away and reached for a couple of small, blank cards from the neat stack at the end of the table. She carefully wrote a message on each, before placing them in the pocket of her handbag. She got up and tidied the mug and plate into the dishwasher. As she left the kitchen, she pushed her chair in, so it was snug and straight under the table. By the front door, she picked up two bouquets of flowers which had been sitting overnight in a bucket of water, and headed out.

She walked at pace along the early morning streets of Highbury, head down, with just an overenthusiastic blackbird for company. She hoped Lloyd had already opened up. She hated to wait outside.

The large, black gates were shut so she stood patiently, trying to make herself inconspicuous, even if her long shadow stretching into the park had other ideas. The forecast had been for another full day of sunshine. Her nerves were calmed the minute she saw him striding over, trousers sagging under his abundant belly, a rogue dreadlock spilling out from under his tall, black cap. *Oh, Lloyd, what would I do without you?* she thought. No words were exchanged. Just the squeak of the heavy iron gate opening between them. They shared a polite nod and off she went into the bosom of the park.

Lizzy had done the walk many times, pacing the pathways, taking in every bench as she went. First up was

Sophia Papadopoulos, 17th May 1951–2nd August 2014 'Our Greek Goddess who loved to sit here and sing along with the early morning chorus'. Lizzy had often wondered what the Greek Goddess's voice sounded like, and how wonderfully exotic and exciting it would have been to be her friend.

Next bench along was Brendan Fraser, 24th July 1981– 22nd December 2019 'Engineer and Elvis impersonator. Clissold Park was his stage'. Lizzy wasn't a huge Elvis fan but was pleased Brendan and Sophia were close – imagine those two doing a duet!

By the main gates was Richard 'Dickie' Edwards, 4th July 1918–13th July 1940 'Spitfire pilot who fought for his country in the Battle of Britain. He loved this park'.

Then Frankie Fontaine, 12th June 1970–9th December 2010 'A star on these pitches, now with the stars in heaven'. Lizzy's Google search had revealed Frankie had been something of a minor legend from the Sunday League football circuit, having once scored sixty goals in a season, but sadly had never made it into the Arsenal youth team.

She strode on in the glorious sunshine, loving the solitude of the empty park. She acknowledged each departed soul with a respectful nod, like a priest blessing their congregation. Every one of them had a story and every one had played out some part of it in this park. Lizzy felt privileged to be in their company.

Today was unusual in that there were two benches to celebrate on the same date. The first was up by the ponds: Dennis Hickley, 19th August 1919–27th January 2015 'Keen birdwatcher who loved the ponds'.

That made Dennis 96 when he died. That's a decent age. Hope I get that old, Lizzy thought. *What did he die of?* The plaques never said, but then why would they? *Cancer? Car accident? Something falling from the sky?*

She'd never really given the benches much thought until Mum had died. The prognosis had initially seemed positive, with the doctors saying her bloated stomach was probably a bit of stubborn constipation and she'd be home by the weekend. But a scan revealed widespread cancer and poor Mum was gone within six weeks.

In the days after the funeral, Lizzy had walked the park alone, thinking of all the great times they'd had there, and started to read the dedications on the benches in detail, imagining these souls living on in Clissold Park. She'd been looking for something to focus on, a distraction from her grief, and slowly but surely, she'd hatched a plan to remember not just Mum, but everyone in the park.

In total, there were ninety-seven benches, including those in the rose garden by Clissold House. None appeared on the Ordnance Survey map or any maps she'd found online; she'd needed to document each and every one herself. Over several weeks, she'd walked the park and noted down every bench, its location and plaque details, which were then inked onto the master map in the kitchen.

At first, she'd pieced the map together on a couple of printed-out sheets of A4 but soon realised that was not going to work. The map needed to be bigger to do the job justice. And rather than drawing the benches on, which became a little scruffy and blotchy as the ink bled into the paper, she took a trip to Ryman's and bought an extra-large pack of coloured pins to represent the benches. A much neater solution.

The next task was to figure out if the benches were active or dormant. When she'd started out, she'd had no idea how involved the project would become. Not just in the physical sense of walking the park, recording the names and dates of the dead, but also this next stage – possibly the most important of all – figuring out which souls were actively being remembered and cared for. And which had been forgotten.

The last thing she wanted to do was encroach on other people's grief. Lizzy hated fuss or awkward situations. So, to be completely sure, she had begun to observe the benches, checking for signs of activity (outside of snogging teenagers), for heartfelt displays of people missing loved ones.

She decided on a simple colour code: green pins signified active benches – fresh flowers and cards spotted regularly, not just on birthdays and anniversaries, but other occasions such as Christmas and Easter. These benches were to be left well alone. The living were very much remembering their dead, and she saw no reason to be involved.

Then there were the dormant benches, which were documented with red pins. These were benches where no flowers or cards or balloons or tinsel ever appeared; these were the ones that needed her. The map started to take shape. It had an unusual beauty she loved, the red and green pins creating random patterns of colour on her kitchen wall.

However, she soon realised there was another detail required before she could celebrate these forgotten souls:

the exact dates of their birth. Quite a few dormant benches were extremely sparse with detail: Yvette O'Keefe, 1940–2012, for example, wasn't much help in telling her exactly when Yvette was born. She'd toyed with the idea of merely placing flowers on these benches at the beginning of the year, but quickly discarded it for being a bit crass and just not right.

A visit to the National Archives births, marriages and deaths website was her next task. Over a week, she methodically scrolled through pages of information and dates, getting to know the navigation of the site and eventually matching the exact names and dates with the red pins on the map. Additional Google searches unearthed more information which gave Lizzy a more rounded picture of these departed souls that she was going to celebrate.

The night she finished, she shut her laptop with a sense of pride and excitement; she could finally get out there and celebrate everyone's birthday. She rewarded herself with a large gin and tonic. Mum would've approved.

This morning, all Dennis Hickley had to show for his big day was a splash of bird shit on his plaque. Lizzy cleaned away the white goo with a tissue, before gently laying the flowers to the left of the plaque, petals facing the pathway. Always the same. She reached into her handbag and retrieved the handwritten card, setting it next to the flowers: 'Thinking of you'.

She thought of Mum again, and one of her classic expressions: "Enjoy the good days, because there'll be a bad one just around the corner." It was one of many Mum had repeated to Lizzy as a child and throughout her life, and no doubt also told the kids at Stoke Newington School where she'd worked as a dinner lady. 'Dinner lady' was a strange title, never really doing justice to the huge character her mother was.

She was always there for any and everyone who needed a chat or a warm word, especially little Lloyd, who was the cutest but naughtiest of the lot. Little Lloyd was now big Lloyd the park-keeper, who'd been a constant on their visits to the park ever since. Mum and Lloyd always had a chat whenever they saw each other, and reminisced about what a tearaway he used to be.

When Mary died, Lloyd was shaken. But when he'd heard about the idea of Mary joining the other memorial benches in the park, he was delighted. Ever since that day of unveiling the bench by the tennis courts, he always took a moment and remembered her. He'd told Lizzy he felt honoured to be involved. There was a bottle of bubbly and much reminiscing, ensuring they lived up to another of Mary's mottos: 'The dead only truly die when the living stop thinking of them'.

Lizzy closed her eyes, shutting out the world, and said a little prayer of remembrance. She always felt lighter the minute she'd laid the flowers. She didn't need 'likes' or to be shared or featured in the local paper. It was just an anonymous act between her and the deceased. She quietly wished Dennis Hickley happy birthday and continued with the second bouquet in her hand. And a small knot in her stomach. This was the most important bench of the year.

She dug a fingernail into one of the lily stems, before walking with a brave face towards the bench that sat just behind the tennis courts. Mary Joan Emma Depla Todd,

19th August 1931–30th September 2022 'Mother, sister, daughter, friend and bon viveur, the park will miss you'. Or 'Mum'.

It had been an easy decision to place the bench by the tennis courts after all those years spent on court eight. At the time, it had felt like a bit of daughter-and-mum fun on a Saturday morning. But now it felt huge in her mind, and she'd have given anything for another rally. Never did she think she'd miss Mum hitting yet another serve into the net with her usual quiet refrain of "Bugger", quickly followed by a much louder "Sorry, darling!".

They'd played tennis well into Mum's eighties. They knew they weren't very good (hence choosing the end court), but they loved the way it brought them together and kept them fit. And they always had a laugh when Wimbledon came around. Every Tom, Dick and Harriet clogging up the courts for two weeks, random balls flying into court eight, interrupting their games at regular intervals. "Sorry", "It's our first time", "We never normally play!" and a million and one other excuses. They smiled and waved and rolled their eyes when they left the court, enjoying a couple of tins of Pimm's. Great motivation for the amateur tennis player.

But it wasn't just the tennis court where she thought of Mum. The picnics near the reindeer pen had been another part of growing up by the park. Her earliest memories were of feeding the reindeer bits of hard-boiled egg and recoiling as the large male jutted its antlers at the fence, trying to get his long, pink tongue onto the yolk.

The thing she missed most, though, wasn't the tennis or the picnics; it was the companionship, the chat, the small stuff – like spotting the now grown-up Lloyd in his buggy over on the far side of the park, debating how long it'd be before he did a drive-by and slagged off Rob.

Mum was a caring, fun-loving character who came to life in the company of others. She kept up to date with friends and never forgot to send a birthday card with many exclamation marks!!! She was a confidante to so many. She was always there, ready with one of her expressions: "What's for you won't go by you", "The best way round is through" and possibly her most eccentric, as she justified a huge extra dollop of cream on her apple crumble or a second gin, "It's the Belgian in me!" which seemed to cover many of Mary's excesses.

Sitting on the bench now, Lizzy wished more than anything that Mum was next to her. Sharing one of their moments. Possibly some champagne decanted into a coffee flask ("Keeps it chilled, darling!"). They'd get comfy next to each other, have a sip and a giggle, waiting for who would comment first on the tennis on court eight, occasionally shouting "Bravo!" if a crisp volley went in.

The bench was a much better idea than a gravestone. She and Mum had never been keen on graveyards, which they found a bit grim. Parks had much more life in them. They'd chatted in the hospice and agreed to go for the posh option, lattice ironwork at both ends and lion-head armrests, their golden faces full of life and energy: that was Mum all over.

Sunlight warmed the side of Lizzy's face. She didn't want to leave.

A robin landed on the other end of the bench and watched as she diligently placed the flowers to the left of the plaque, petals facing the pathway. She took the card from her handbag and carefully leant it next to the flowers before heading for the gate.

Thinking of you, always.

"Happy birthday, Mum," she said gently, "Happy birthday, everyone."

SEPTEMBER

The coin

The silver coin was wedged firmly into the trunk of the large oak. It had clearly been placed there by human hands; the small, shiny disc pressed into a gap between the dark columns of bark. Embossed on the shilling was a man's profile, King George III. A high forehead, protruding eyes, large nose, thick lips and a dimpled chin surrounded by the words '*Georgius III Dei Gratia Rex*'.

Facing the coin, some twenty paces away, was another man, Lord Clissold. Dressed in a ruffle-fronted shirt, blue tailcoat and crimson cravat, he cut a dashing figure. No one feature was perfect, but taken together, the brown eyes, straight nose and thick, wavy hair made for an attractive man. He eyed the coin with menace, pistol held casually by his side. Sunday mornings were his favourite, as it meant target practice or 'pistols at dawn' as he liked to call it, at the back entrance of his beloved Clissold House.

He'd never actually fought anyone with a pistol at dawn, let alone hit the coin in years of trying. But that wasn't going to stop him. In fact, the idea of target practice was the driving force to get him out of his grand four-poster bed, rouse the dogs and be shooting by eight.

The coin was always the last target. He'd start with empty bottles of port from the scullery and large pieces of fruit from the pantry, basically anything his servants could find that he could easily hit with one of his duelling pistols.

With a nod, the long-barrelled weapon would be passed by one of his staff, who hated this tiresome charade. Sunday mornings were their only chance to have a lie-in, but unless Lord Clissold was away, that luxury rarely happened.

To make matters worse, Lord Clissold would invariably be hungover and wobbly with his aim. The previous night had been another of the legendary punch nights. The latest brew comprised apples and pears from the park, stewed with several bottles of claret and rum from the cellars. The dark liquid smelled like a sickly sweet affair, but judging by the singing and dancing that went on long into the night, it was his finest yet, the evening ending as it always did, on the roof terrace, where the dregs consumed the dregs.

This morning, near-silence reigned along the corridors of Clissold House, all eight bedrooms humming with gentle snoring. As ever on such occasions, Lady Clissold was nowhere to be seen, wisely having decided to go away to the country for the weekend.

He held the pistol in front of him, hand gripping the polished wood handle, one eye half closed, focusing on the coin. At his feet lay Jack and Frieda, his loyal spaniels, who would do anything for their master. They looked up obediently, waiting for the signal to give chase: "Just a minute, my beauties. Wait... wait."

His finger wavered over the trigger, and the air was suddenly filled not with the crack of a gunshot but the squawk of crows swooping down from the eaves of the house, dark flashes cutting through the morning grey, four of the black birds landing on a nearby bench.

Lord Clissold turned and stared angrily at his servants as if they were somehow to blame for the activities of the wildlife in the park. The staff looked down at the ground, hands behind backs, wishing to God he'd get on with it.

Bang!

The crows gave flight again, the dogs' ears pricked up, and Lord Clissold lifted his head to peer through the wisps of gun smoke at the tree beyond.

The coin was gone.

He ran over, dogs in close pursuit, adrenalin mixing with the alcohol still coursing through his veins. He leant down, eyes scouring the turf for the coin. Or at least fragments of it. The dogs followed suit, noses hovering over the ground.

"Come on, my beauties. Where's our King?"

But much as they tried, they found nothing. Not even a piece of shrapnel. The staff were commandeered to undertake a thorough search along the banks of the nearby New River, but it was a fruitless task.

For the rest of his life, Lord Clissold would talk about this moment, with every passing year embellishing the story, talking about his direct hit on the King, his act of treason, claiming to be the sharpest shot in Stoke Newington. But alas, with no actual proof.

***

Janet was on her knees in the reindeer pen, hunched over, hands deep in the soil, desperately trying to find the root of the Japanese knotweed. It had been a problem earlier in the summer and now it had really taken hold along the perimeter of the reindeer's habitat.

She'd put on her high-vis jacket and cordoned off the area before getting stuck in. Thankfully it had rained, making the ground, previously rock-hard from the intense heat of early summer, much more malleable.

She sensed someone or something behind her and turned to see Donner and Blitzen sniffing at the soles of her boots.

"Get back, you naughty boys! Shoo!"

A moist, black reindeer nose nudged the pocket of her jacket, sensing a tasty morsel inside. Janet was having none of it and outright refused, irritated they'd breached the barrier.

"No. You'll have your treats later. Now shoo, go away."

She knew she ought to get professionals in to treat the knotweed with glyphosate but was worried how it might affect the soil and her beloved herd. Rob and Lloyd had mentioned getting a mini excavator and doing the whole pen, but that too would be disruptive. They were a sensitive bunch and easily spooked.

One more big tug, she thought, *and back to the shed for a coffee.*

She didn't mind Lloyd; she found him good company, a man happy in his own skin. But Rob was irritating, and she always tried to avoid him. Rob was an Arsenal fan and Janet supported Spurs. She wasn't football crazy, but as a child she'd loved being with Dad at White Hart Lane, sitting high on the big man's shoulders, holding on for dear life. Dad would scream his lungs out, his steaming raspy breath would rise so she'd be watching the beautiful game through his mist. She still had a picture of Steve Perryman somewhere at home; he was her favourite.

But it was more than football rivalry. They were fundamentally different people: Janet was happy to do her own thing, stay in the background and mind her own business. She was friendly but with a private side. Rob was loud, brash, full of himself and always interrupting people, which was Janet's pet hate. But she tried to be civil in his company, if only out of respect for Lloyd.

With one last heave, she managed to release the root. The momentum sent her backwards like an oversized Weeble, rolling in the mud, but heroically managing to hold onto it. She brushed herself down and held up the ugly root as if it were the head of John the Baptist, tendrils for hair and a stone in the middle for a nose. She picked it out and on closer inspection realised it wasn't a stone, but a coin.

She thought it was a 50p, or maybe a £2 coin. She gave it a rub, expecting to see the Queen, but was met by a chubby-looking king instead. She wandered over to the fountain for a breather, washing the coin in the water. It was slightly bent, no doubt damaged over its years in the ground, she thought. After a couple of good wipes with the cuff of her uniform, she popped it into her pocket and headed back to her shed.

She felt tired, but good tired, satisfied she'd done a job. Her herd would be safer now and the pen looked a lot neater. There was no sign of Rob or Lloyd, so she settled down with a coffee. She leant back and enjoyed a moment of solitude before she felt something digging into her fleshy left buttock. The coin.

She retrieved it and held it under the bare light bulb to get a better look. The face on the coin was old, a stern-looking king; *certainly not our Liz*, she thought.

The expression was strange too; the slight bend on the coin had pulled up the sides of the figure's mouth, creating a warped smile, making the sovereign more welcoming than he should be. This appealed to Janet. She gave the King a smile, before stretching up and wedging him firmly into the gap between the wall and the ceiling of her shed.

***

The computer screen was reflected in Rob's large, ill-fitting glasses. He hated wearing them. They made him look like a knob, but they were a necessary evil for the admin part of his job. This morning he was sorting out his shifts when an email notification pinged on the desktop: 'BBC filming in Clissold Park'.

Rob immediately opened it. His eyes darted across the first couple of sentences and, without thinking, he shouted out to no one in particular: "Oh my God. We're going to be on TV!"

He read further down the page (probably the most he'd read for quite some time) and proclaimed in the same hysterical fashion: "It's from the BBC. Someone called Hannah says the *Antiques Roadshow* are coming. They're coming here. To Clissold Park. This is it. Lloyd. Lloyd!" He banged on the shed wall. "It's our moment."

Lloyd heard the noise and the shouting but didn't react. Instead, he bent down and made sure the buggy was charging properly before looking up at the grey sky, hoping the day would cheer up. He'd grown accustomed to Rob's overexcited outbursts, which were both endearing and irritating.

They'd been working together in the park for years now and had learnt to endure one another's foibles. Lloyd had to accept Rob's childlike excitements and obsessive behaviour, while Rob had to accept Lloyd's laid-back attitude to life that bordered on narcolepsy.

Lloyd waited a beat, thinking maybe Rob was reading the wrong email. But on the second outburst, in which Rob mentioned the *Antiques Roadshow*, Lloyd's ears pricked up. He loved that show, especially Fiona Bruce, whom he had a bit of a crush on. He popped his head in, trying not to look interested. "What's that, Rob?"

"Mate, look here, read this!"

Lloyd retied his dreadlocks before stuffing them back under his hat and read the email. It looked official, he had to admit, but he didn't want to encourage Rob so just nodded and left. He wandered over to the buggy, the small charging light now flashing green. Then he set off, thinking of the BBC's flagship Sunday-evening programme, and wondering if he could get a selfie with Fiona.

***

The same email was opened in another shed by the reindeer pen, with a less enthusiastic response. Janet's interest was quickly crushed by the thought of the park being overrun by a film crew, stressing out her herd. But worse than upsetting her reindeer was the thought of what being on national television would do to Rob.

"Knock, knock!" Lloyd popped his head in.

"Oh, hi, Lloyd," she replied. "Grab a seat." Lloyd sat down on the table, which groaned slightly.

"You seen it?" he asked.

"Yep," she replied in a resigned tone.

They looked at each other for a moment, before laughing.

"He's going to be unbearable!" exclaimed Janet.

Both knew what was coming. They didn't actively dislike Rob. On the contrary, they admired his enthusiasm for law and order in the park. It was just moments like this when they knew he was going to turn into hyper-Rob, which wasn't good for anyone.

"Shall we get ice cream?" asked Janet.

Janet needed something comforting. She and Lloyd often bought choc ices from Tina's ice-cream van on Queen Elizabeth's Walk when Rob wasn't around. It had become a routine break in their days earlier in the summer.

"Bit early?" Lloyd wondered.

Janet smiled. She knew it was, but the thought of it made her feel a bit better. Lloyd got up and patted her affectionately on the shoulder. "Don't worry, Jan, it might be more fun than you think." She looked up at the coin before rereading the email.

***

"Hi there. Nice to meet you, Hannah. I'm Rob, the park-keeper of Clissold Park." Rob had his chest puffed up, hand out, beaming at Hannah Schumacher, the BBC producer.

"Nice to meet you, Rob. What a lovely park you have here."

"We do our best," replied Rob, trying to appear humble.

He took a step back and bowed ever so slightly. "Shall we?" he asked, indicating the passenger seat for Hannah to step into, as if it were a Roman chariot rather than a dusty park-keeper's buggy. She hopped on and they drove towards Clissold House.

Lloyd and Janet were watching from a safe distance where they could hear the conversation, nursing cups of coffee and eating Rob's Hobnobs, marvelling at his levels of obsequiousness. "We do our best," they mocked, giggling like a pair of schoolkids, enjoying the spectacle of 'Lord Rob' masquerading as master of the estate.

They heard a beep and turned to see, by the main gate, someone on a moped, waving to them.

"Deji!" said Lloyd and walked over.

Deji removed his helmet and greeted Lloyd with an outstretched palm. "Here he is! Lloyd, the lord of the manor!"

"How you are doing, Deji?" replied Lloyd. "You're back on your wheels."

"You know it. Thanks for getting those bastards."

"You're very welcome," replied Lloyd. "But I have to say it was all your sister's work. You need to thank Abi big time."

"I have loads. Plus, this weekend I'm taking her to Wingstop in Leicester Square as a treat. I've even got that stinky horse of hers a bag of sugar lumps."

"Nice. She'll be so happy."

Deji replaced his helmet, signing off with a muffled, "Come round for chicken later."

***

"On your left the reindeer pen, to your right the old paddling pool and ahead, of course, Clissold House, which has been in my family for over three hundred years." Rob was giving Hannah the grand tour.

"Really?" Hannah looked at Rob, surprised.

"Nah, only kidding. Nice gaff though, isn't it?"

Hannah admired the stunning Grade II listed building with its expertly restored architecture, floor-to-ceiling ornate windows on all sides and a stunning roof terrace, all set in tranquil manicured gardens.

"What's it used for these days?" asked Hannah.

"Well, there's a café on the ground floor and then there's your posh dining rooms for weddings and private events upstairs."

"Can we get up on the roof?" continued Hannah. "It'd be great to do a shot from up there."

"Absolutely, we can fix that for you, no problem," Rob replied, knowing full well he had no jurisdiction whatsoever. But he was going to go along with it for as long as he could, which was for about another forty seconds, as he had spotted Sebastian the local councillor approaching to take Hannah off to discuss the options for filming.

Rob headed back to the shed, desperately trying to think of a way he could get on the show and tell his mates he'd made it onto national television.

***

The next morning, Rob got into work early and went over to Janet's shed. He tried the door, but it was locked. He cupped the morning light from his eyes and looked in through the small window. He saw the coin wedged in between the wall and the ceiling.

His mind began to race, imagining himself on national television, holding the coin delicately in front of the cameras, discussing its value with Fiona Bruce, who'd no doubt be charmed by Rob's banter, throwing her head back in laughter at yet another of his park-related quips. He tried the door again but no joy.

"Can I help you?" Janet's stern voice took Rob by surprise, but he tried not to show it.

"Morning, Janet. How are you?"

Janet stared at Rob's face for a moment.

"Are you OK, Rob?"

"Never better."

Janet frowned at this surprise greeting at such an early hour and unlocked the door.

"You excited about the filming?" asked Rob.

"Not really. You?"

"Can't wait. I think it's going to go really well. I got talking to some of the TV crew last night and they said this is the best location they've ever had."

Which you no doubt took all the credit for, Janet thought.

"That's nice," she replied.

Rob perched himself uninvited on the edge of her table, adjusting his side parting, ensuring the neat blond flick swept perfectly across his forehead. "You got anything for the show then, Janet?" he asked in faux-interested fashion. "How about that coin you found the other day? Got to be worth something?"

"What coin?" Janet replied, getting more irritated by the minute.

"That one up there." Rob nodded at the coin. "Lloyd told me."

Janet made a mental note to have a quiet word with Lloyd about how their private conversations needed to remain private.

She reached up and removed the coin before holding it in her hand, studying the King's face. "I'm sure it's worthless."

"Well, you never know, Janet. You got to be in it to win it."

She thought about giving it to him, just to get him out. It was as clear as day that that was why he was there. But she decided against it.

"Well, Rob, I'd love to chat, but I have eight reindeer and three goats relying on me, so I'd better get on." She put the coin back and stood in front of Rob, shooing him out as if he were one of her herd, before shutting the shed door.

Janet had read the same sentence in her Marian Keyes book five times and still hadn't taken it in. She couldn't stop thinking about the coin. It had started to roll around her mind. And now it was interrupting her bedtime reading. So many 'what ifs'.

What if the coin was worth nothing? She'd be embarrassed.

What if it was worth something? Even a few hundred quid would be nice.

What if it was worth more, like thousands? She could treat Dad and take him on holiday for the first time in God knows how long. Or fix the bathroom. Or take herself away. Maybe go and see her old friend Natalie who'd gone to live in Ibiza, who was always telling her to come over.

For all these 'what ifs' whizzing round her brain she blamed Rob. But, to be fair, he was right: why didn't she go for it? What was there to lose? *Sometimes you're just way too stuck in your ways, Janet Evans*, she thought.

She put Marian Keyes down, pushed the purring Tabitha off her chest and reached for her phone, typing into the search bar 'old silver coin valuations'.

***

Rob was in make-shit-happen mode. It was still a couple of days before filming, but he'd been in the park since 6am. He'd done all the bins, making sure every scrap was cleared away. He'd scrubbed the love heart graffiti off the base of the water fountain and even given the statue of

Lord Clissold a little polish, wiping away the bird shit from his boot.

Hannah had told Rob that he needn't tidy up too much, as they were only planning a couple of wide shots of the park itself, then the rest would be close-ups of the presenters, the experts, the public and their antiques. Rob nodded and smiled, not listening to a word. He gulped down his black coffee, crunched through his fourth Hobnob of the morning and went off, checking for holes in the perimeter fencing and signs of fresh dog poo on the pathways.

Lloyd was trying to remain calm. He'd taken to pouring a slightly larger glug of rum into his morning coffee to take the edge off things. He had decided to steer clear of Rob in the build-up to filming, letting him boss the buggy while Lloyd remained close to the shed, on hand in case something was needed. The crew had runners for all sort of tasks, but Lloyd felt he could help. And was perfectly placed when the heavens opened just as Fiona Bruce was rehearsing her introduction for the show. Lloyd had spotted the dark clouds and had already got the umbrella from the shed.

And so there he was, just out of shot, keeping Fiona dry as she sat on Derek Underdown, 13th March 1955–27th August 2015 'He loved it here', doing her introduction to camera, which needed a couple of takes. Fiona's first attempt was drowned out by a flock of parakeets who swooped down from the eaves of Clissold House and landed on another nearby bench.

As Fiona was finishing up, Tony, the local café owner, walked past, arm in arm with Astrid, Eric their beagle at their feet, sniffing the cables. Astrid leant into Tony, hugging him closely and whispered in his ear, "Look, Tony, it's Fiona Bruce getting ready for the *Antiques Roadshow*. Doesn't she look elegant?" Tony made what he thought was an enthusiastic noise from the back of his throat. "I love her scarf," continued Astrid. "We need to get her into the café for a cup of nettle tea. Raise our profile on the socials." Tony rolled his eyes and cuddled Astrid tightly.

"We don't need Fiona Bruce, my darling. We've already got our local celebrity right here," and gave her a gentle kiss on the cheek.

Eric looked up at his smooching owners and started to bark.

***

Janet had had a disturbed sleep. She'd spent way too long looking at antiques websites and had all sorts of vivid dreams, one of which involved her dad, a waterslide in Ibiza and an enormous spinning coin. She felt groggy and needed something stronger this morning than her regular coffee, so she headed off to Muddy Puddle on Church Street for one of their double shot Americanos.

As she wandered past Clissold House, she saw large, white tents being erected in front of the mansion, each branded with the *Antiques Roadshow* logo. It was a hive of activity: people with clipboards, cables on the grass, food stations set up. She viewed it all with a mix of hope and horror, the 'what ifs' crowding back into her mind.

She saw the buggy approaching, Rob at the wheel

giving her a smile, eyes wide open. She had to look away and made her exit out of the park. This was the hyper-Rob she didn't like. She needed her coffee.

After seeing Janet leave the park, Rob turned the buggy sharply towards the reindeer pen and drove up to her shed, before heading inside. In her tired haze, Janet had forgotten to lock up. Rob snuck in and reached up, taking the coin, cupping it in the palm of his hand, staring directly at King George III.

"You, my friend, are going to make me famous."

He'd never been keener to open the work laptop, adjusting his glasses as he quickly searched for Jonny Benton-Jewels, the local antiques dealer, who often frequented the park with his little sausage dog. Rob jotted down his mobile and, within minutes, had arranged to meet up.

Lloyd was watering the geraniums by the old bowling green with a watchful eye. The minute Rob had showed interest in Janet and her coin, he knew something was up. As Rob left Janet's shed, Lloyd noticed he was still wearing his glasses.

Rob, totally oblivious, walked with purpose across the park to meet Jonny in Tony's Café, or rather the Forager's Café as it was now known. Lloyd decided it was time to act and went back to the shed to wait for Rob's return.

It didn't take long; Rob returned within twenty minutes.

"Put it back," Lloyd said in a stern voice.

"Eh?" Rob tried to appear dumbfounded.

"You know what I'm talking about, Rob. I saw you. You took Janet's coin and went to see that Jonny bloke in the café. I was watering the geraniums; I saw it all."

Rob tried to deny it, but he knew he'd been caught when Lloyd pointed out he'd left the laptop open, on Jonny Benton-Jewels' website. He was embarrassed and replaced the coin, before skulking off, throwing his glasses on the side.

**

"Welcome to the *Antiques Roadshow*, coming to you today from Clissold Park, Stoke Newington in Hackney, North London."

"Cut!" shouted the director. "Thank you, Fiona. Very good. Check the gate please and let's move on."

"Just a moment, Toby," said Fiona to the director. "Can we do one more, and get those roses in shot?"

Fiona pointed to the flowers just over her shoulder. "The pinks and reds really are beautiful. Set my scarf off nicely."

"Of course," replied Toby, "one more please, people!" he shouted as the crew got ready to shoot again.

Just out of shot, Lloyd was grinning so much it hurt. All that tending and care and the recent addition of horse shit from Hope had paid off – his roses were going to be on national television. *Look out, Deji,* thought Lloyd, *I'll be round the chicken shop later tonight!*

It was Friday. Filming day. And the first shot was already in the can. The weather was grey, with rain forecast for later on. But the crew were prepped to move inside the tents if need be.

Lloyd had already been in to see Janet and the coin. He wasn't going to tell her about yesterday's incident with

Rob, but rather focus on getting her ready for her big moment today.

"I'm just checking you're OK, my dear," he said softly.

Janet looked at Lloyd and all she could think of was ice cream.

There was a knock on the door. It was Hannah. "Janet, could you come now please. We're going to film you and the others. This is just to see if you've got something that genuinely merits a slot on the show."

Janet dipped her hand into her handbag.

"If your coin is good enough, we'll film you later this afternoon, so this morning is a bit of a dummy run." Janet applied some lipstick, a quick check in her pocket mirror and she followed Hannah out.

"Break a leg, Jan," said Lloyd.

"Ice cream later?"

"Of course."

***

Standing in line, Janet felt silly. Unlike everyone else wearing their nice summer outfits, she was wearing her work clothes: drab dark-green park-keeper's outfit, heavy black boots and the deeply unflattering hat, all of which the producers had specifically asked her to keep on, to give an air of authenticity. 'The park-keeper who unearthed a gem' was definitely on their list of by-lines for the show.

The queue wound its way towards the valuers' table in front of Clissold House. Locals stood patiently in line with their offerings, one or two harbouring dreams of fame and fortune. Others, such as Kenroy with his box of

Arsenal football programmes, were a bit more pragmatic, merely happy to be there enjoying the mid-morning sunshine.

Just in front of Kenroy was the tall, upright figure of Tony from the café, whose hand was resting on the top of a large picture frame leaning against his thigh. Kenroy caught Tony's eye and offered a polite smile and an outstretched hand. "Kenroy."

Which was reciprocated: "Tony. Nice to meet you. I think I've seen you around the park."

"I'm the early walker," said Kenroy.

"That you? I've seen you from my bedroom. I've always wondered who the man in the bright-red top was. So dedicated."

"Not out of choice, my friend. I have to do it. Doctors' orders. Got to up my cardio to keep the cholesterol down."

"Oh, cholesterol. Dreading my levels will have gone right up again."

"What's the picture?" asked Kenroy, peering over at the picture frame.

Tony lifted it up to show the image of a large piece of orange peel winding around a debonair figure dressed in a red polka-dot outfit, holding a bottle of Campari aloft, all set against a black background.

"Not a fan myself," said Kenroy in slightly dismissive tone.

"Of the poster?" replied Tony with a raised eyebrow.

"No, sorry, that's lovely. I mean Campari – so bitter!" Kenroy pulled a face.

Tony nodded and replied with a knowing grin. "You get used to it after the first ten years."

Kenroy chuckled, looking down at his box of Arsenal football programmes.

"More of a smoothie man myself these days," offered Kenroy. "Although, don't get me wrong, on a night out it's rum and Coke all the way."

Both men were enjoying each other's company with the warm sun on their backs.

A lull in the conversation was filled by another hopeful queuer, Janet, who was behind Kenroy, looking at his box of programmes.

She couldn't help herself. "I remember when Charlie George broke our hearts at The Lane." Kenroy turned.

"Oh hi, Janet. Didn't see you there. Yeah, those were the days. I dug these out last night. Thought they'd be worth a punt."

"Well, you never know, Kenroy. Gotta be in it to win it."

"Yeah, you're right."

"What have you got, Janet?" Kenroy asked.

"Oh, just this," replied Janet, retrieving the coin from her pocket. Kenroy squinted at King George.

"Strange-looking fella."

"Yeah, I know," replied Janet. "I'm not really sure whether that's a good or a bad thing."

"Get you with your magic coin!" Janet turned upon hearing a familiar voice behind her.

"Abi!" Janet's face lit up upon seeing her reindeer-feeding assistant from a few weeks back. "You OK, my darling? You look gorgeous. Love the hair." Abi flicked her braids and smiled.

"What you got there?" asked Janet, looking at the

large bag in Abi's arms. Abi opened it up to reveal a pair of Ghanaian ceremonial tribal masks.

"They've been under Mum and Dad's bed gathering dust for years. Thought I'd see what they're worth."

"Got to be in it to win," said Janet again, surprising herself at how quickly she'd adopted Rob's expression, which she now felt most at home with. Janet studied the hand-carved wooden masks, admiring in particular a proud rhinoceros strolling across the male mask's forehead. "Hopefully one of us will get lucky."

***

The morning went well for the producers. They were after a mix of stories, from the potentially large valuations that viewers loved, to the human-interest stories, which were even better if they involved locals. By lunchtime they knew who would be featured.

Janet was still none the wiser about whether the coin was worth something. But hope was definitely growing, as she'd been told she'd made it through to the filming in the afternoon. Kenroy and his programmes hadn't. Apparently, there were many men who'd brought along football memorabilia. The producers were much keener on a collection of vintage skateboards.

***

John Foster, one of the stalwarts of the *Antiques Roadshow*, lifted the optical glass up to his eye, bringing the coin into view. He had a good, long look, taking in the profile of King

George III, the marks on the chin, feeling for a moment with his thumb how strong the indentations were.

Janet wasn't enjoying how long it was taking and wanted to sit down; the harsh interior lights were making her sweat, and she could feel her uniform starting to stick to her legs. Her mind started to drift to the 'what ifs'.

John Foster looked up with a bit of a sigh, without trying to give too much away. "It is most definitely King George the third, which in itself isn't a great find." He held out the coin so the camera could see, but also allowing Janet in shot.

"These marks here are the key."

Janet's heart was sinking. *I knew those bits of dirt would ruin it*, she thought. She felt stupid, hating Rob, hating herself, waving goodbye to the holiday with Dad and the new bathroom. She stared into the distance, wishing she was anywhere but there. She heard one of the producers quietly say off camera, "Janet, focus on the valuer please."

"These marks here at the bottom…"

She couldn't help herself and interrupted, "Yes, I imagine it's not worth anything, so I'm going to go now."

"Not so fast, Janet," replied John with a half-smile. "Just a minute."

It was an awkward moment, but the director and producers kept the cameras rolling, knowing full well this was TV gold.

"As I was about to say, these dark marks… are, in fact, very exciting."

A small murmur amongst the crowd.

"These marks are not deep-seated dirt or soil, but in fact tiny fragments of a lead bullet. And lead embedded in a coin like this means it would've come from an old pistol." Janet was confused, but was now leaning forward, looking directly at her King.

John continued in authoritative manner. "I've located a painting that shows Lord Clissold holding a duelling pistol in front of him, aiming not at a rival, but rather at a tree, with his dogs by his side."

After having seen Janet's coin earlier in the day, John had known it was special and had dug into his archive material to find a reference to the painting from the late 1700s.

"This picture shows his morning target practice. I'd say this is one of the coins that he used to shoot at and was lost in the grounds. The lead shot embedded in the coin is proof of such, and unequivocally dates the coin to pretty much exactly 1779, which is the rarest year for these coins. It may well have been shot not far from where we're standing now, possibly at one of those trees over there." The crowd turned and stared at the large oak tree by the New River.

"So, although people say a damaged coin is worth less, in this case it is the damage that makes the coin worth more. All of which means this coin would be valued at a considerable sum."

Janet was staring intently at the King's face, the strange, warped smile and the marks on the chin. She was mesmerised, but was brought back into the room, or rather the tent, by the sound of John's voice. "…Janet, you're looking at around £5000 for this little chap."

She put her hands to her mouth. A glint of a tear appeared in her eye. The cameras were catching it all. The producers were smiling, already planning a little drink on the roof terrace of Clissold House. The audience gave a spontaneous round of applause.

Janet didn't know what to say, but managed a quiet, "Would you just excuse me for a moment?"

Lloyd had been too nervous for Janet to go along with her to the filming, and had instead stayed in his shed, listening to a bit of Radio 2.

She half-walked, half-ran back, opening the shed door to Lloyd's hopeful face.

"So, are we good, Janet Evans? Are we still getting ice cream?"

Her smile said it all.

"Lloyd, we're going to have all the ice cream!"

And she shrieked and clapped her hands, and they hugged in the tiny shed, Lloyd's hat knocking the bare light bulb as they created one big happy human.

They walked slowly towards Tina's ice-cream van by the far gate. Janet stopped for a moment and said, "Lloyd, you carry on. I just need a minute."

Janet did an about-turn and walked back towards the main entrance of the park and the statue of Lord Clissold. She stood directly in front of him, looked up into his face, tracing the contours of his slightly chubby cheeks up to his warm, friendly eyes, and said quietly, "Thank you, Lord Clissold."

OCTOBER

The dead party

Rob used the pliers to twist the two sections of mesh fence tightly together, closing the hole. "That should stop the little bastards," he said under his breath, giving the fence a final tug before heading off to check the gate on Queen Elizabeth's Walk.

It was Halloween, which for most of the locals was one of the best nights of the year. An evening of trick or treating, carving pumpkins, lighting fires, letting off fireworks and making memories.

None of which interested Rob. What interested Rob was that no one broke into Clissold Park on his watch. He had a blemish-free record and wasn't going to lose it to some feral thirteen-year-old letting off an Excalibur artillery shell on the tennis courts.

He could just imagine the scene the next morning: Lloyd, leaning back in his chair, sipping his rum-infused coffee, asking in that relaxed but loaded tone, "Yo, Mr

Security. What happened last night? I thought you were 'sealing the park'?" The words 'sealing the park' would be laced with sarcasm.

The thought of messing up gave Rob the shivers. So, today was crucial. He was 'all over it', as he liked to say. A park-keeper with purpose, making shit happen. Or rather not letting shit happen.

Rob loved a task. Something to give him a sense of achievement. And he particularly loved having a task when Lloyd wasn't around. On days like these, the park became his kingdom. He could feel his heartbeat increase whenever he was on a solo shift, desperate to make the most of his time. A modern-day Lord Clissold running his estate.

And woe betide anyone who got in his way, especially this morning in the fully charged buggy, 1.5kW of power under his right foot. The electric buggy which, once again, Lloyd had let go flat last night.

Sometimes Rob wondered if Lloyd was up to the job. The forgetfulness, the alcohol in the coffee, the poor timekeeping. It wasn't that different ten years ago when Rob had started. As a rookie park-keeper he hadn't wanted to push his luck and tell Lloyd what to do, but he'd never forgotten that first Halloween when things had gone properly 'Pete Tong', as he liked to say: fireworks throughout the night, drunken kids, traumatised animals, even a blaze in the woodlands causing untold damage to small birds' habitats.

Ever since, there'd been a ban on events or any activity on Halloween, leaving 5th November as the only official party night. Which suited Rob to a tee. Every year he'd mark 31st October on the work calendar with his big red pen – 'Rob all day' – so Lloyd knew well in advance he would not be needed.

As he headed back to the shed for his coffee (black, one sugar, Hobnob on the side), he passed one of the many benches dotted around the park: Mary Joan Emma Depla Todd, 19th August 1931–30th September 2022 'Mother, sister, daughter, friend and bon viveur, the park will miss you', and thought he felt something on the back of his neck.

He couldn't be sure what it was. A fly? A droplet of rain? He spun round, but there was nothing. He looked up at the sky which had a strange aura, dark, ominous clouds tinged with a strange orange glow. It reminded him of those moments in films just before the aliens landed. He felt off balance and momentarily held onto the back of the bench, hand covering Mary's plaque, steadying himself.

And then it passed. He felt fine. In fact, he smirked to himself, thinking, *Nah, you prick, there's nothing wrong. It's just those whisky chasers from last night in the Highbury Barn.* Reassured by his hangover, he returned to the shed and put the kettle on.

He decided to send Lloyd a picture of his morning's work: 'OPERATION FORT KNOX COMPLETE. THE PARK IS SEALED!'. The usual thumb emoji came back.

The rest of the day passed without incident. By dusk it was time to lock up. He did one more circuit, driving down the centre of the pathways, holding onto the steering wheel in straight-arm pose as if he was some big shot.

He double-checked all the possible entry points and locked the gates. No one was getting in this park tonight.

They emerged from the darkness in eerie silence, stooped figures skulking across the park, seemingly oblivious to each other. More and more appeared, traversing the space in random formation, the nomads of Clissold Park.

The reindeer shifted uneasily in their pen, eyes darting around the darkness, aware they had company.

The figures started to go their separate ways. One walked off to the ponds, another to the tennis courts, another to the fountain. And then they would stop, journeys over, arriving at their destinations. The benches. Their memorial benches, that bore their names and dates of birth and death. The benches that their loved ones had paid for and visited hundreds of times in their honour. The benches where flowers were laid, and gifts offered at Christmas and birthdays.

And as they settled onto their benches, a subtle change occurred. The ghost-like figures became more substantial. They came to life, appearing like every other visitor to the park, regular human beings enjoying their visit. And, for them, this was the most exciting visit of the year: it was the dead party in Clissold Park.

***

Rob sat by the window in the Clissold Park Tavern with his pint dead-centre on the beer mat. The pub was decorated for Halloween, with cobwebs on the windows, fluorescent skeleton skulls on the ceiling and, on every table, a plastic pumpkin with a smiley face. All completely ignored by

Rob who was attempting the sudoku from the *Metro* newspaper. He could normally do the elementary one. He knew it was easy, but the neatly completed matrix proved he had some semblance of intelligence outside of being a park-keeper.

He took a large gulp of fizzy beer and looked out towards the park, now enveloped in darkness. *All quiet on the Western front*, he thought. *Let's keep it that way.*

For a moment, he thought he saw a glow through the trees. He leant forward, moved a cobweb from the windowpane to get a better look, but the number 141 bus wiped his view and by the time he looked again it was gone.

He took another swig of beer and returned to the puzzle.

***

They were a mixed bunch, like a random fancy-dress party through the ages. Not that any of them cared or could do anything about their appearance. They'd returned to this world as they'd left it, their fashion sense and everything else frozen in time.

By the main gate there was Richard 'Dickie' Edwards, 4th July 1918–13th July 1940 'Spitfire pilot who fought in the Battle of Britain. He loved this park'. He sat calmly on his bench, with the zebra crossing flicking on and off over his shoulder, throwing intermittent light across his boyish face. Dickie was just twenty-two when he died. He looked proud and content in his uniform, holding his brown helmet and goggles on his lap, patiently waiting for the evening to begin.

He leant forward and saluted the figure on the next bench along: Brendan Fraser, 24th July 1981–22nd December 2019 'Engineer and Elvis impersonator. Clissold Park was his stage', who gave a huge theatrical bow back. One of the main characters of the west side of the park, Brendan adjusted his Elvis wig and glasses, ready for a performance later that night.

Next to Brendan was Sophia Papadopoulos, 17th May 1951–2nd August 2014 'Our Greek Goddess who loved to sit here and sing along with the early morning chorus'. Sophia was a lively soul, resplendent in her long, flowing nightie. She carried herself magnificently, a grand woman, easily over six foot, her towering frame matched by the power of an operatic voice that could span four octaves.

Each bench revealed another character. By the water fountain, wearing boxing gloves and shorts, sweating profusely with cuts around both eyes, was Floyd Williams, 5th February 1998–19th June 2020 'It's not the years in your life, it's the life in your years'.

By the ponds were Dennis Hickley, 19th August 1919–27th January 2015 'Keen birdwatcher who loved ponds'; Jimmy the Geordie, 4th October 1966–18th February 2020 'NUFC forever!'; and Francois Murphy, 28th July 1983–9th October 2018 'Loved this park'.

There were new recruits too, up by the tennis courts: Keith Atwell, 18th June 1950–17th March 2023 'Happy times spent here with Poppy the dog', who'd had one of the most bizarre deaths in the park's history, and Mary Joan Emma Depla Todd, 19th August 1931–30th September 2022 'Mother, sister, daughter, friend and bon viveur, the park will miss you'.

The oldest and most revered of all the benches was for the original owner of the park, Lord Clissold, who not only had a bench but his very own bronze statue by the main gates that welcomed visitors on their way in. Dressed in a frock coat with turned-down collar and wide lapels, hip-length sleeveless waistcoat, crimson cravat and breeches, he epitomised the dandy fashion of the late 1700s. At his feet were his trusty spaniels Jack and Frieda, tails going like mini propellers, aware something exciting was going to happen.

The park even had a couple of celebrities: Dennis Norden CBE, Writer and Broadcaster, 6th February 1922–19th September 2018 was sitting quietly on the bench by the pond, next to his beloved wife, Avril Norden, 10th April 1921–3rd July 2018 'Old is when the only thing you can do fast is get tired'.

With everyone now in, rumours started to go round of where the party would be. Lord Clissold's? Sophia's? Or perhaps the new girl, Mary Todd's? Her bench was right by the tennis courts, plenty of room to spread out…

***

Rob had nearly finished the sudoku when he got a text from his mate Nigel, whose flat directly overlooked the park: 'LIGHTS SPOTTED IN PARK, POSSIBLE KIDS GOT IN?'.

Rob liked Nigel. He was a man after his own heart. Living so close to the park, he was Rob's eyes and ears when he wasn't around. Nigel had a particular aversion to fireworks. His brother had lost a finger during a display when they were kids and ever since he had been super vigilant on nights like these. He never let his boys, Soli and Otis, go near them. Rob told the barmaid he was popping out for a minute and not to take his drink.

He peered through the fence, shining his iPhone torch for a better look, but was greeted only by tree trunk silhouettes and the rough outline of the pathways.

He half thought about leaving it: there was clearly nothing going on. Maybe Nigel had imagined it. But Rob being Rob, he couldn't. If there was even the remote chance someone had breached his defences, he needed to know about it. And sort it.

He reached for the keys and let himself back in. He checked all the places he knew kids would hang out – the animal pens, the woodlands, the graveyard, around the fountain – but he found nothing.

Suddenly, his torch caught something, a pair of dead-looking eyes staring right back at him, cold silver ovals holding the beam of his torch. *Gotcha, you little bastard*, thought Rob. It took him a moment to realise it wasn't a feral teenager but a large fox, which soon scurried off into the night.

With nothing else to see, he turned around and headed back to the pub, texting Nigel: 'ALL CLEAR'. But then he heard it. A huge explosion from the tennis courts, followed by a massive cheer.

***

From a distance, it looked like a classic gathering. Rob had seen these many times in the park, most commonly by the fountain where men from the local hostel would gather on a warm evening, drinking miniature bottles of spirits and having a sing-song. Harmless fun, which Lloyd let go, but Rob was always wary of. However, this was bigger than that. In fact, this was bigger than anything he'd ever seen. A huge gathering, maybe one hundred people. There was drinking, laughing, music, dancing, all around the new bench by the tennis courts.

As Rob got closer, he could see they were a disparate bunch: adults, teenagers, old folks, dogs. There was even a bloke dressed as a Spitfire pilot, complete with helmet, boots, goggles and pristine white gloves, which Rob had to admit seemed very realistic. *Maybe it's one of those Secret Cinema events*, he thought. Despite these thoughts going through his mind, he held his resolve: this had to stop.

"Oi, right, stop this! Come on, all of you, go home. This is an illegal act."

No one noticed. They carried on as if Rob wasn't there. Jimmy the Geordie was in full party mode, shouting to Dickie the Spitfire pilot over the music in his broad Newcastle accent: "How the fook did you make that canny explosion?"

Dickie replied in his finest King's English: "Secrets, dear boy, war secrets. I could tell you, but then I'd have to kill you." They looked into each other's eyes and burst into laughter, Jimmy shouting, "I bloody love you, Dickie man!"

Rob tried again.

"Right, come on, you two. Stop that. Parties are illegal here on Halloween and I have the authority to shut this down." He leant in and tried to break the men up, muscling his short, bulky body in between them, but he couldn't get a grip. In fact, his hand seemed to pass right through them, and he ended up nearly falling over. He held onto the back of the bench, which thankfully was rock solid, and regained his composure, Mary Todd coming to his aid for the second time that day.

"Now stop playing silly buggers, you two!" He went in one last time with even more purpose, but once again he passed through the jovial men, now singing a rude song about Hitler.

Rob tried to regain some composure, adjusting his side parting and brushing his blond hair across the top of his head before flicking a few rogue leaves from the front of his trousers.

He turned his attention to the music coming from court eight, the last of the tennis courts adjacent to the pathway. He could see a small crowd of people singing along to what looked like Elvis Presley in the middle of the court, performing a pretty decent version of 'Hound Dog'. *This is getting more bizarre by the minute*, thought Rob. He stomped over to grab Elvis by his big, sequinned collar, but again it was as if it wasn't there, Rob's hand grasping at thin air.

Amongst the crowd of revellers enjoying the music, Rob did a double-take and spotted Keith, the same Keith he'd rescued from the frozen pond at the beginning of the year. Instinctively he shouted out, "Keith mate, it's me Rob, over here!"

No response. Very unlike Keith, who was always so polite and engaging. *Something's clearly not right here*, he thought.

Rob returned to the bench and took a breather, finding himself next to a jolly-looking old lady who seemed to be orchestrating events. She cupped a hand to her mouth and shouted over to Elvis: "Come on, Elvis, let's have a song for the new girl!"

Elvis gave Mary a theatrical bow. "Coming up, Mary!"

"Mary?" Rob looked at the old lady. She must be Mary Todd who had died late last year after a short battle with cancer. Rob recalled Mary's daughter, Lizzy, had held an unveiling ceremony for the bench, attended by Lloyd who had known Mary from her days as a dinner lady at Stoke Newington School.

Mary seemed to be on a mission, cheering on the music and dancers while simultaneously helping Lord Clissold, sat at the other end of the bench, make his infamous punch. Mary was chopping up fruit and plopping it into his large silver urn, while slyly dipping her finger in for a taste. Lord Clissold leaned across Rob and held out an ornate silver ladle to her. "Mary, my dear, what do you think?"

Mary took a sip, pretending she didn't already know how good it tasted, "Delicious, my lord. Maybe a bit more rum?" Lord Clissold adjusted his crimson cravat and laughed.

"Mary, I'm so pleased you're here! You're exactly what this park needs, a breath of fresh air." Mary smiled and gently ran her fingers through her white, wavy hair to give it a bit more body. She wanted to look good for her first night.

The alcohol was doing its thing, and she got up and grabbed Sophia Papadopoulos from her dance partner, Keith, politely asking, "May I?" before launching into a set of spins and skips that took Sophia by surprise. "Come on, Sophia!" enthused Mary. "Plenty of life in us yet!" And with that, she stood on Sophia's sequinned slipper, resulting in a shriek and cackles of laughter.

Rob stayed put, watching it all dumbfounded from the bench. He couldn't work out if he were dreaming or not. He rubbed his eyes, checked his side parting and clicked his knuckles – all things that normally helped him reset. But the bizarre scene was still there, playing out in front of his eyes. It was a jolly group, people genuinely happy to be here, no malice or aggression, just the joy of, well… being alive.

The fun wasn't confined to the humans: the dogs were having a night of it too, racing around, chasing sticks thrown by Keith.

Rob could feel himself gently sinking into the bench, muscles relaxing, letting go and welcoming in a different sort of energy. His mind started to question things: *Why stop people having fun? Sometimes it's better to let it go. No amount of fence security and patching up of holes would've kept this crowd out.*

Slouched and smiling with a hand calmly laid on top of the lion's head armrest, he admired Mary, ninety-one years young, twirling and giggling, nudging Dickie next to her, holding her steel tankard aloft as if it were the greatest night of her life (or death).

I need some of that, thought Rob.

He got up and, although he now knew no one could see him or even acknowledge his presence, he didn't care. "Come on, Elvis!" he shouted. "One more!" And as the opening chords to 'All Shook Up' blasted out, Rob got in amongst the throng and started to dance himself, taking in the heady bouquet of the rum punch and losing himself to the moment. He even shimmied over to Mary and Sophia, attempting to drop down and up in the style of The King, nearly cricking his knee. Mary and Sophia raised their tankards to each other. Rob raised an empty hand to toast the dancing ghosts.

The dogs started chasing one another across the under-elevens' football pitch, racing past a couple of foxes, having the time of their lives. The party seemed to be reaching a climax as Rob saw Mary return to her bench and climb up onto it.

Mary adjusted her hair once more and cleared her throat in an effort to get people's attention, but to no avail. She resorted to tapping her ring finger firmly on the side of Lord Clissold's metal tankard, as if she were the best man at a wedding. But everyone was too engrossed in dancing and chatting, and ignored the best woman.

Rob felt frustrated for Mary, and noticed Lord Clissold get up next to her on the bench and reach deep into his inside jacket pocket for something. A pistol. Lord Clissold held the weapon high above his head, cocked, ready to fire, a Davy Crockett figure staring the crowd down with his weapon. Rob thought, *You could get five years for possession, having one of those in Hackney*, but didn't think now was the moment to mention it.

The sound of the gunshot echoed around the park and no doubt up and down the streets of Stoke Newington. *Ghosts or not, surely someone heard that?* Rob thought.

The piercing sound had the desired effect. Peace and quiet replaced singing and dancing and, but for a little stumble from a tipsy Geordie, all eyes were on Mary up on her bench. "Thank you, Lord Clissold," she said politely, before addressing the crowd.

"Hello, everyone. You all having fun?" The question was answered with loud cheers. "I'm Mary and I just wanted to say thank you. I am the new girl, as you all know, but you have all welcomed me so much I already feel like one of you, which I suppose I am now." She adjusted her hair once more before looking out across the sea of bright, lively faces. "Not forgetting Keith Atwell of course, who's even newer than me. And whose bench is right next to mine." Mary indicated the adjacent bench. "Nice to know you, neighbour. Where are you, Keith?" An arm was raised in the crowd as Keith and Mary gave each other a wave.

"Keith and I feel incredibly lucky to have met you all. And we're very much looking forward to getting to know you even better tonight – what's left of it – and in the years to come. My wonderful daughter, Lizzy, did this for me," she pointed to her bench, "like all your loved ones did for you, and so I feel they are the ones we should be toasting tonight. They've never forgotten us. So, we should never forget them. A toast. To the living, from the dead!"

And with that, they all raised their drinks as one. "To the living!"

Rob decided to leave them to it and subtly drifted away. He was exhausted and not a little elated, but knew somehow it was time to leave. He needed to clear his head and walked over to the ponds. As he passed the large willow trees and rounded the bend by Queen Elizabeth's gate, he noticed there was a chill in the air he'd not felt before. He turned his collar up and continued walking. Within a few more paces, he nearly lost his footing on the pathway, which was iced over with a smattering of snow. It hardly seemed possible, but the evening was taking yet another funny turn. As he approached the second pond, he could see his breath and feel his teeth starting to chatter in his mouth.

And that's when he saw him – a large figure in a dark jacket and top hat, skating on the frozen pond in beautiful wide arcs, without a care in the world.

His first instinct was to berate him, his mind racing back to January and how angry he had been that someone would break the park rules and skate on the pond. But he stopped himself. He was in a different space now. It didn't bother him. In fact, if he was honest, he enjoyed the spectacle. It was just what he needed after the madness of the party.

He was completely still, mesmerised by the skater's poise, grace and balance. He turned around to see if anyone else was enjoying the show, but he was totally alone. The skater came nearer and nearer, seemingly oblivious to Rob's presence, executing a perfect spin which woke a resting moorhen who scuttled off into some nearby reeds.

Rob couldn't help himself and started clapping, not just at the performance he'd just seen, but also to get his circulation going and warm his freezing hands. There was no reaction. The skater was lost in himself, turning and heading off behind the island of trees in the centre of the pond.

"Bloody hell," said Rob to himself as he decided enough was enough. Time to get back to sanity and his pint in the Clissold Park Tavern. He headed towards the south gate and started to warm up, turning his collar back down and feeling steadier underfoot, the pathway now completely dry. But, as he reached the gate, he could see the pub was now pitch black, with just the beer pumps offering a gentle ambient glow inside the deserted building. He looked at his seat by the window, and there was no pint or newspaper in sight.

There was a stillness in the air. No people or traffic. Just the occasional scrap of litter dancing across the road. His eye was caught by the green digital clock outside the chemist's: 6:54am. The night had gone. It felt like only a minute ago he was locking up. And now he was standing in the middle of the road, like a vagrant on a lost highway, unsure where to turn.

He rubbed his head, ruffling his blond hair, the neat side-parting giving way to a sticky-up unkempt mess. He looked back into the park. The sun was starting to break through the trees. His shift was due to start in six minutes.

A fox scampered into the park. Rob followed, head down, trudging directly towards the hut, where he went in search of Lloyd's rum.

***

"You OK, Rob? Mate, you OK?" Lloyd was genuinely concerned. He'd started out jovial, laughing at his fellow park-keeper for looking a dishevelled mess. But he'd quickly realised something was up.

Rob had his head in his hands. He hadn't noticed Lloyd come in. Rob looked up slowly, pained bloodshot eyes blinking like a vampire trying to avoid the sun. He looked back down at his rum-infused coffee and took a large gulp, responding in what he hoped sounded a confident and lively manner.

"I'm fine, mate. Never better."

Lloyd sat down and sniffed the air.

"You don't smell fine. What the hell were you drinking?"

Rob didn't respond. Too many questions. Too early. He pushed back his chair and got up, wincing a little as he put weight on his knee, before heading out, trying not to look Lloyd in the eye.

They walked in silence past the buggy towards the tennis courts. As they approached Mary Todd's bench, Lloyd caught the same pungent smell he'd detected inside the hut, a fruity alcoholic odour: "Rob. Be honest. Did something happen here last night? Did people get in?"

"No, mate. It was all quiet." Rob ran his fingers through his hair in an attempt to re-establish some semblance of order. "Couple of foxes, that was it, mate. Nothing happened. It was totally dead."

As they continued towards the ponds, a Spitfire emerged from a dark cloud and flew directly overhead, performing an acrobatic roll over the tennis courts. Rob looked up and gave the plane a salute. Lloyd didn't notice a thing.

NOVEMBER

The ballistic brothers

Soli hung upside down, blood rushing to his head, impish blue eyes staring at his little brother, Otis, in the bunk below, willing him to wake up. Soli's body swung gently, mousey brown hair tickling his sibling's chubby cheeks. No response. He lowered himself further, flicking the full fringe across his face. A couple of sweeps did it. Sleepy eyes met excited eyes. Soli spoke quietly, but with steel in his voice.

"It's time."

Otis was up in a flash, barely able to contain his excitement, pulling his jeans over his Spiderman pyjamas before grabbing his trainers and standing at attention by the door, waiting for Soli to give the signal for the mission to begin.

They retrieved the large canvas bag and Dad's gardening gloves from the shed before grabbing a pack of wine gums from the kitchen cupboard, and silently walked through the house. Soli delicately closed the front door behind them, letting the latch click with the deftest of touches, before running down the road with his accomplice, giving the local fox a friendly wave as they went.

Clissold Park was silent and still. A blanket of fog was gently lifting from the carpet of autumn leaves. Nine hours previously, the place had been like a war zone. Huge booming detonations reverberating around the park, rockets flying high into the night sky at colossal speeds, and an endless cackle of bangers, all to the delight of the gathered crowd.

The brothers had never witnessed such an event in the flesh. If they were lucky, their father, Nigel, would give them a brief viewing from his bedroom window that overlooked the park. But never for long.

"Five minutes, boys, then lights out," was his mantra. Then he would return on the dot and close the curtains, ending the show. Over the past couple of years, they had become more curious as to why they weren't allowed to have fun like other families in the neighbourhood. They seemed to be the only ten-and twelve-year-old boys not allowed out on one of the main nights of the year.

"Why can't we go?"

"What's so bad about it?"

"Why aren't we like other people?"

They even got to begging: "Please, Dad!"

Until they got the sobering answer. It wasn't something that had happened to their dad, but rather to his brother, their Uncle Adam. The two families had been at a large firework display back in the seventies when a rocket fell as it went off, firing straight into the crowd just 20 feet away.

It had sliced the top of Uncle Adam's thumb clean off; the screaming was something their dad never forgot. But in a way, Adam was the lucky one. A boy behind him had been blinded. Since that day, everything had changed. No fireworks, ever.

They were shocked and sad for Uncle Adam. But they were also curious boys who just wanted to have fun. They desperately wanted to be part of Bonfire Night, in any way possible.

Otis wiped the last crumb of sleep dust from his eye and gazed across the park, itself still waking up. No dog walkers or joggers, barely any wind. Just the fifty-five acres stretching out in front of them, full of possibility.

It was their kingdom, for the next half an hour at least, before the park-keeper started his rounds. They'd got in through a new hole they'd found in the fence on the far side of the park. They worked quickly and efficiently like a pair of sniffer dogs, retrieving the exploded carcasses and placing them carefully with gloved hands (one each) into the canvas bag.

Otis had made mental maps of where the colourful munitions were landing the night before when they were watching from Dad's bedroom, shouting out locations as if co-ordinates from the battlefield. Soli had gone one step further and plotted the trajectories on the back of his geography book.

The football pitches were first. Large, open spaces where the fireworks gave themselves up easily on swathes of autumn leaves. It was exhilarating and urgent work, and they were handsomely rewarded. The deeper they went, the more they found.

ROCKET THUNDER by the pond.

EXCALIBUR ARTILLERY SHELL on the tennis courts.

ANGRY BATS in the children's playground.

Otis spotted one of his favourites, MOONSHOT! on the inside of the reindeer pen. He leant through the wire fence, desperately reaching down to the bright-red firework, but his arm fell agonisingly short. He tried a couple of times before giving up, accepting this might be one that got away.

Soli, meanwhile, was taking a breather on the other side of the park, sitting on Frankie Fontaine, 12th June 1970–9th December 2010 'A star on these pitches, now with the stars in heaven', eating a wine gum. As he was thinking about going for a second, possibly a green one, which was his favourite, he heard a shout from by the water fountain.

"Soli... here!" shouted an excited Otis. "This is the one. Remember I said from last night?"

Sure enough, there, in the middle of the flower bed, slammed head first into the dark soil, was the evidence of the last huge explosion they'd seen before Dad abruptly ended the show.

Otis reached over much more easily this time and gently eased the thin wooden stick out of the ground, as if he were an archaeologist discovering a centuries-old weapon, rather than a £19.99 rocket that had sparkled for no more than a few seconds.

The ground released its treasure, crumbs of mud flicking onto his white trainers, but Otis barely noticed. The two-foot-long rocket had his full attention. Soli ran over to inspect it, slowing to a walk as he took it all in.

BALLISTIC BOMB.

The drop-shadow behind the thick red letters on the yellow background made the words pulse like they were alive. Impossibly exotic, exciting, forbidden. If Dad could see this… a tingle of fear and excitement flew up Soli's spine.

They studied the blackened base where the fuse had been lit and crept its way to the tightly packed gunpowder that sent the capsule into orbit before setting off a series of explosions in a breathtaking, predetermined sequence. A magic moment when huge, red spikes pierced the night sky over the park, before vanishing seconds later, as if it had never been there.

They placed this final prize in the now-bulging bag and headed home. It was their biggest haul. Last year they'd got forty-three. This year they had blasted through the sixty barrier.

As they approached the park gates, Lloyd the park-keeper appeared at the wheel of his buggy and for a moment blocked their path. Their hearts jumped. Lloyd acknowledged them with a gentle tap of the peak of his Rasta cap.

"Morning, boys. Doing my job for me?"

The brothers were silent, petrified. They knew they shouldn't be in the park this early. If it was Rob, the other park-keeper, they would be in trouble. But Lloyd knew what was going on: he'd seen them here before and had an inkling their dad was one of the strict ones.

"Don't worry. You're all right with me, boys." And with that he was gone. And so were the boys.

***

Like a pair of late-night stop-outs, they crept through the house to the back garden, and breathed a sigh of relief. Heroes back home, welcomed by the resident robin, twitching on the roof of the shed.

Soli got to work, retrieving the large dust sheet from the shed, spreading it out by the back wall where no one could see. He threw it in the air a few times, loosening the creases to create the perfect blank canvas. Then he meticulously laid out the dead fireworks one by one, like priceless pieces for an art exhibition.

Otis looked on without interrupting, choosing to scoff a wine gum himself and have a good pick of his nose. He knew his older brother well enough not to interrupt this moment.

The rockets always took centre stage, their leggy sticks lording it over the angry little bangers pushed to the edges. Then there were the anomalies – the strange new shapes that came every year: this year's favourite was a stubby twin-pack, looking like a chocolate milk carton with a fuse on top.

Soli carefully placed the final banger and stood back, admiring the collection, knowing the best bit was still to come.

The sniffing.

Initially, they had just wanted to be at a display with other families admiring fireworks. It didn't seem too much to ask. But, because of Dad, they had been forced to take another path, which opened the door to not just collecting dead fireworks but inhaling them.

It had happened by accident that first year, when they'd gathered armfuls of spent fireworks and held them up in the air, mimicking how they would've flown through the night sky.

They'd inspected every detail – the colours, the typography, the small print 'Not to be supplied to any persons under eighteen years of age' – and their nostrils soon got involved. One whiff of the burnt gunpowder was all it took.

This sensory pleasure soon took centre stage and became the very heart of the ritual.

Soli went straight for BALLISTIC BOMB: raising it to his pert freckled nose, inhaling deeply, like a master sommelier savouring the notes of a fine wine. Burnt gunpowder never smelt so good. It was from another world, the dark skies. Illicit, illegal perfume. He passed it to his brother, who accepted it reverently as though it were a shisha pipe. He too sniffed from the hole at the blackened base, taking in the explosive residues.

They put it back in its place and Soli gave his brother the nod to proceed. Otis went for a banger. Soli shook his head and smiled. Every year it was the same. Otis loved the bangers; he'd be on twenty a day if he could. Otis shut his eyes and sniffed, trying to outdo his brother with his performance, ever the showman: his neck gently swaying, head dancing, eyes closed, in heaven.

On it went, both diligently taking it in turn to work their way through the haul. Every burnt-out carcass was sampled by the ballistic brothers and their well-trained nostrils, mentally logging their favourite bouquets.

And then it was done. The ceremony over for another year.

Soli wiped a giveaway black smudge from his little

brother's nose. Otis lifted the canvas bag. It felt like there was still one left. He opened it and the morning sunlight illuminated something shiny and red at the bottom.

Otis froze.

Soli leant over and saw what his brother saw – a bright-red, pristine firework. Their very own live rocket. Something they'd only ever dreamt about. And now it was here.

Soli picked it up out of the bag. His brain was racing, considering what would happen if they let it off right now. They'd need to find something to light it with. He knew Dad kept a box of matches in his jacket which he wore when he went out to the pub. Maybe Otis could creep back in and get it?

He'd played this moment in his mind so many times it felt surreal now that it had arrived. He shut his eyes and imagined the sequence: the scraping of the match along the coarse edge of the box, the flare of the flame which he'd let settle for a moment, before lighting the fuse which would burn tantalisingly, before the whoosh of the rocket flying into the sky, climbing invisibly higher and higher until finally revealing itself with a climactic explosion, bright-red spikes darting across the sky in dagger-straight lines. The sound of the explosion would reverberate around the neighbours' back gardens and, of course, when the patterns in the sky were gone, they'd be left with the intoxicating smell of burnt gunpowder.

But then came Dad's stern words. He could hear him once again tell the story of Uncle Adam and he knew it wasn't right. It wasn't worth it.

He gently put it back in the bag before looking his brother in the eye, saying calmly, "We don't need this one."

DECEMBER

Janet's little helper

His face was pressed hard against the wire fence, button nose fitting neatly into one of the square gaps. The more he leant in, the more the hard, black mesh sank into his soft, olive skin. Not that he noticed. His mind was elsewhere, busy brown eyes darting around the pen, following the extraordinary beasts, fixating on one in particular. The big one with the spiked horns on its head. That was his favourite already. It looked cool and scary, like something from one of his X-Men comics.

He'd seen llamas back home, but never anything like this. Suddenly, another appeared, an even bigger one; its ears twitched for a second, before it ran straight at the first one, head down, hooves thumping on the hard, frosty grass. They locked horns; parakeets in a nearby tree gave flight at the harsh clatter of bone on bone. It was a brief but fierce tussle. A moment later it was over, and they went their separate ways.

He peeled himself away from the wire and turned, expecting to see a crowd behind him, equally impressed. There was no one, except Beth his nanny sitting patiently on Priscilla Quinn, 1948–2007 'Clissold Park was her special place'.

"The big one's the troublemaker, always wants to fight."

The voice came from just inside the fence, a middle-aged woman in a park-keeper's uniform, carrying a metal bucket and a warm smile.

"What is it?" the boy asked.

"What's what, my love?" Janet replied, slightly flummoxed.

"What is the animal?"

"That's a reindeer. Have you never seen one before?"

The boy shook his head, still in a mild state of awe.

"They've been here ever since the park was opened back in…" Janet paused, "1790-something, and I've been looking after them ever since." She smiled at her joke, which the boy completely missed. Although the truth was, she had been looking after the animals in the park for nearly thirty years now, which was still quite a feat. The line of questioning continued.

"Do they have names? Are you their owner?"

Janet peered through the wire fence, looking down at the inquisitive little character. She dealt with many questioners during the festive season. But this little chap seemed different: the way he looked, how he spoke, the accent – was it Spanish? Portuguese?

"His name is Blitzen. He's a right one, and the other one was Prancer…" she strained her neck, trying to see the back of the pen, lifting the peak of her green cap, "there's eight of them in total but you can't see them now, they're all behind the screen." The boy nodded; no more questions for a moment, just cold breaths.

"And may I ask, what is your name, young man?"

The boy diligently wiped his hand on his trousers before squeezing it through a gap in the fence.

"My name is Santiago Gonzales. Nice to make your acquaintance."

Somewhat taken aback by the formality and wonderful pronunciation, Janet paused before reciprocating with her own introduction, taking the boy's warm little hand in hers. "And my name is Janet Evans. Pleased to meet you."

"What are those things on their heads? Are their brains in there?"

Janet beckoned him over to the end of the enclosure and together they read the official Hackney Council information board on Fallow Deer, before Beth took Santi home.

***

"Do they talk to each other? Who's the oldest? Are you a deer doctor?"

It was 7.45am and she'd not even had a cup of coffee. She'd never had anything like this before. Still, it kept her on her toes. She'd revised a bit in bed last night, Marian Keyes usurped by *The Reindeer Handler's Yearbook*, sensing Santiago might become a regular fixture for the next few weeks.

"Yes, they do talk to each other, but we humans can't hear them. They have their own special way of communicating. The oldest one we've ever had was Reggie. He was sixteen before he passed away last year, bless him. What was the last question? Ah yes, me. Well, I'm officially known as the livestock manager of the park, but it's easier to just call me the park vet. I'm basically the mum to all these wonderful creatures." She pointed to the bird cages, chicken coop and goat enclosure on the other side.

Santi nodded, absorbing the information.

Janet noticed a bright-red object nestled tightly against the base of the wire fence. She bent down and grabbed it: a dead firework. Holding it up for Santi to see, she read the name out loud: "MOONSHOT! Looks like it missed the moon and shot into our cage, Santi!" She looked to see if the joke had landed. Nothing.

Santi focused his attention on Janet, the way only kids do. It was something about her eyes that did it, vibrant green, they seemed to sparkle against her pale skin. And the white hair that framed her kind, welcoming face. He was captivated and for a moment imagined she must have something to do with Father Christmas.

"You OK, Santi? Shall I tell you what they got up to last night?"

Janet loved making up stories about the deer, the secret world that she created and shared with the small people of Clissold Park. One year she'd told a tale of how she had to tie an eager reindeer to the ground to stop him flying off too early. She'd laid the rope out first thing the next morning as 'proof' of the story. She was quite proud of that one.

Of course, there was a limit to membership of this club. Up to around eight years old was the cut-off. After that, it wasn't quite the same. Janet could spot the non-believers a mile off; standing further back, some on bikes half-listening, chucking in a few barbed comments, sniggering, looking at their phones. But she wasn't there for them. The ones at the front were her babies.

Janet was everything Santi's mother wasn't. Pale, old, a bit plump, but she listened and was interested in him. Santi's parents both had busy jobs. His father, Jose, was a systems analyst at Google, recently relocated from Lima to London. As the new guy, he worked long hours and was obsessed with data, his boffin nature making him question anything that couldn't be proved by one of his beloved charts or algorithms. Santi's mother, Paola, had a busy job as a civil rights lawyer. They adored Santi and managed to juggle jobs, bath-time and dinner together thanks to Beth their nanny. But they always felt there was never enough time to give Santi their full attention.

***

Santi's main curiosity was about the antlers. Why did they have them? What were they made of? What happens if you cut them off? He finished his bowl of Cheerios as his mum rushed out of the kitchen, putting her coat on, eating a piece of toast and kissing the top of his head all in one movement, shouting, "Christmas in four days, *bambino!*" Her speedy exit blew over the Christmas cards on the table.

Santi picked them up, holding onto the one with a large reindeer that seemed to be staring directly out from the card at him. He stared back, mostly at the antlers, before Beth told him it was time to go. He grabbed his satchel and off they went to school. That afternoon the question of the antlers was soon forgotten when James Crabtree wrote on Santi's maths book: 'Reindeer can fly'. It nearly made his head explode.

***

"Santi. Santi. Santiago?"

His teacher, Miss Campbell, was staring directly at him, her voice getting louder and more irritated.

"Yes, Miss Campbell."

"What is so fascinating about the sky out that window, Santi? Is there a fronted adverbial out there?"

"No, Miss, sorry. What's a fronted adverbial, Miss?"

***

The minute the bell went, he was off to see Blitzen, dragging Beth with him. His excitement spot – a small, red birthmark just beneath his left eye and a mood indicator for all to see – was bright red as he raced across the park. Janet was cleaning the bird cage, humming along to 'The Rivers of Babylon', when she was rudely interrupted by more questions from Peru:

"Is it true? James Crabtree says they can fly!"

Janet had been waiting for this moment. She walked over to the gate, took off her gloves and folded her hands in front of her, as if she were about to give a sermon to her congregation.

"Why yes, of course they can fly, but only once a year. That's why we have to look after them, in preparation

176

for Christmas Day. They need to be in tip-top condition ready to help Father Christmas deliver the presents." She surprised herself at how convincing it all sounded.

Over Santi's shoulder, kids and parents laden with shopping listened attentively. She had them in the palm of one hand, metal bucket in the other.

As the crowd dispersed, parents left to do the rest of the explaining on the way home, while Santi remained with Beth. Janet could feel his need for companionship and crouched down on her haunches, looking into his cherubic face. "If you come back in ten minutes," she whispered, "I'll introduce you to them."

"You mean in there?" He tried not to shout with excitement.

"Yes, I mean you can come in and say hello to Prancer and Blitzen, but only when everyone else has gone, OK? And only if you get your parents' permission. And Beth brings you. How far away do you live?"

Santi pointed to the row of terraced houses just beyond the tennis courts.

"Perfect. Come back at 5:30pm."

He was gone before she'd finished the sentence.

***

"They can fly! They can fly! James Crabtree told me in maths and Janet told me too!" Only when he was in the centre of the room did Santi realise it was pitch black, the slice of light from the hallway picking out the tinsel on the Christmas tree and his far less sparkly father horizontal on the sofa.

"Papa, it's amazing! Believe me, Papa! They can fly!"

Jose opened his eyes to see his son bouncing in front of him.

"Oh, Santi. Hello, little man. Can we do this later? Papa has a migraine."

Santi raced through to the kitchen, where Paola was still in her coat, talking on the phone, hand up already to keep Santi at bay. He dropped his satchel onto the table, knocking over the Christmas cards. He took the reindeer card with him and wandered upstairs. In his bedroom, he looked across the park and counted down the minutes to 5:30pm.

***

As she got ready for Santi's return, Janet's mind drifted back to her childhood and the happy times spent with Mum and Dad. As an only child, she'd loved having both of them all to herself. It was like they were a little gang, rarely separated.

She always wondered why modern couples spent so little time with their children when they bring such joy. Why have them in the first place if you're just going to farm them out to after-school clubs and nannies? But she didn't dwell on it too much. Life is different these days and she felt so lucky at what she'd had. Christmas was always the best. If it snowed, Dad would bunk off work and take her and Mum to Ally Pally and, with hearts in mouths, they'd toboggan down the sheer slopes at incredible speeds, racing to the bottom. Before doing it all again. Those were some of her most precious memories.

If she could create one such moment for Santi this year, she'd be proud.

***

It was completely unprofessional and wrong and against everything she'd been taught. But Janet didn't care. These were special circumstances. And Santi was a special case. They were like a pair of kids up to no good. They stood very still in the centre of the pen and waited patiently until Blitzen wandered over, as long-suffering Beth sat on the bench outside.

Santi stroked Blitzen's speckled brown-and-white coat. It wasn't soft and furry as he'd imagined, but hard and bristly. His hand went up towards the antlers, but Janet shook her head. Instead, he stroked the bridge of the nose and got a little lick in return from Blitzen's large, pink tongue.

Santi and Janet giggled and looked around as if checking for Miss Campbell to tell them off. Santi held out his hand and Janet filled it with red berries from her bucket. Blitzen's tongue returned, this time taking the lot in one great slurp, before bending down to hoover up any spilt morsels on the ground. Santi duly wiped his hand on his trousers.

As they left the pen, Janet got Santi to stand next to Blitzen. She made a strange *coo-ing* noise at the back of her throat which caused Blitzen to lift his head and stand perfectly still as the photo was taken. They locked the gate and wandered over to the hut. Santi was speechless. *Job done*, thought Janet.

"Here, look, he really likes you."

She turned to show the picture on the screen. The top of Santi's head reached just above Blitzen's knee.

***

The next morning, Janet got in early. As she entered the enclosure, she spotted the 'Do not feed or touch the animals' sign and felt a pang of guilt from last night. She wandered into the pen and got a warm welcome from Donner, trotting over for a mouthful of fruit and a drink of water. Janet needed a drink herself and popped to the hut. As she filled the kettle, she spotted a well-stuffed A3 envelope on the table. It looked official, something from head office and definitely not another Christmas card for the collection: sum total three so far.

She opened the package. The blood drained from her face as she read the cover letter. She stared out of the window at the pen. Everything went quiet, as if a massive cushion was drowning out the sounds of the world. She couldn't move, gripping the letter with both hands. The sound of an iron gate being rattled brought her back to reality.

"Mrs Janet, Mrs Janet. Are you OK, Mrs Janet?"

Janet was rubbish at covering her emotions. Her mother said she had a leaky face. You always knew when something was up with Janet Evans.

"Er yes, no. I'm fine, Santi, just tired."

Under the thermal vest, a knot was forming in her stomach.

"Is Blitzen OK? Did he sleep well?"

She couldn't reply. Everything went foggy again. Her

brain was asking a million questions and for once she didn't have the answers. What should she do? She felt responsible for him, his eager-beaver face, the huge eyes all big and hopeful, those grubby little fingers.

And suddenly it happened. She thought of something that wouldn't just make things OK, but would make this possibly the greatest Christmas in the history of the park. The warmth flooded back to her cheeks. The green eyes lit up full beam, power restored. Everything was crystal clear.

"Yes, Santi," she said, new purpose in her voice, "Donner, Blitzen, Dasher, Dancer, Prancer, Vixen, Comet and Cupid all slept like logs, like Yule logs," – another joke wasted on the little man, – "and they are ready for tomorrow. In fact, I'd say this is the readiest they have ever been. Are you ready, Santi?"

He skipped off to school with Beth holding his hand, and Janet returned to the hut, brain whirring. She carefully put the letter back into the overfilled envelope and placed it in the recycling bin outside.

***

She didn't sleep well that night. The ingenuity of her plan versus the sheer idiocy of it had her tossing and turning all night. Not even Marian Keyes could help. Could she pull it off? Or would she bottle it?

At 7:45am the next day, the answer was waiting for her at the gate. But before he could reel off any more questions, she beat him to it.

"So, what do you think is going to happen, Santi? Will

the reindeer fly off to help Father Christmas deliver the presents or will they still be here on Christmas Eve?"

"They're going to fly, Mrs Janet!"

If Janet had had an excitement spot herself, it would've been bright red by now.

"Come by this afternoon to say goodbye and we'll give them some treats."

***

By 4pm there was a crowd of kids and parents outside the pen. Janet was centre stage.

"Good afternoon, everyone. Just to say that as tomorrow is Christmas Eve, the reindeer will be flying off to help Father Christmas deliver presents. So, let's all wish them good luck and give them plenty of snacks for the journey. Thank you for bringing the carrots. It's just what they need."

Of course, Janet knew carrots were the last thing reindeer needed. A reindeer's diet consists of fresh greens, small fruits, oats and the odd bit of bark. But, occasionally, if she was feeling kind, she'd let an illegal bit of food through. Blitzen was partial to a hard-boiled egg in the summer from families enjoying picnics on the grass in front of the pen. And, during the festive season, Janet had to suspend the rules once again for the deluge of Christmas carrots.

They were quite a jolly crowd today, one or two of the adults clearly more relaxed than others, thanks to the Forager's Café mulled wine takeout deal – two cups for a fiver – which seemed to be going down well. The vibrant purple brew was rich and warming, steeped in herbs which Tony, Astrid and Eric had foraged from the woodlands specially for Christmas.

Amongst the faces, Janet spotted a teenage girl with long, brown hair and a bold, beautiful face, who was giving her a little wave. It was Essen. Janet smiled and wandered over. Essen had been one of her favourites when she was younger, always chatting about school and the reindeer. Like Santi now, Essen had been obsessed with Donner and Blitzen and everything to do with Christmas, a girl after Janet's heart, and the bond had remained all these years.

Just behind Essen were her mum and dad. Janet only occasionally saw the mum but knew her dad, Ali, very well. In the middle was tall, skinny Josh, Essen's boyfriend, who'd finally come good after a rocky start. Janet had heard about the moped gang and Ali getting upset but was pleased things had calmed down now. Essen and Josh looked a cute couple. Essen proudly told Janet how Josh was cooking them all a special Christmas dinner to show off his culinary skills.

"I'll believe it when I see it," quipped Ali, who was immediately chastised by his daughter.

"Shut up, Dad. Don't be mean," said Essen. "Come on, Josh," she added, "let's show Dad just what a fine chef you are. See you, Janet." And with that, they left.

Santi waited patiently until the crowd had dispersed further before silently approaching the fence. Beth knew her place by now, and was settled down on the bench checking her phone. Santi reached into his pocket and produced a small carrot, which he reverentially passed through the gap in the fence to Janet.

"For Blitzen."

Janet nodded and then watched him all the way to the tennis courts before returning to the deer pen, checking her watch.

***

That evening, Santi held a pair of binoculars against his bedroom window, straining to see into the park. He adjusted the focus and thought for a moment he saw a reindeer leap up, attempting to fly. There were lights flickering and he saw more than one reindeer jump. He was convinced he saw an old man with a white beard too. He lay down and stared at the night sky through the half-open curtains.

***

The table was piled high with carrots, maybe a hundred of them. Janet studied the orange mountain for a moment, took a breath and dived in, chomping her way through the first one in seconds, breaking it into irregular chunks, like some kind of ravenous beast from a horror film.

She didn't swallow a single piece of carrot, instead spitting out every morsel onto a large cloth on the table. One down, ninety-nine to go. Like a human grater: whole carrots went in, small chunks came out. Halfway through, she took a breather and looked up at the coin wedged in-between the wall and the ceiling of the shed. Or rather where it would've been. Nothing there now, but the £5000 it had sold for at auction had bought Dad a holiday with enough left over to tidy up the bathroom. She still couldn't believe it. *God moves in mysterious ways,* she thought. Especially in Clissold Park. She felt a little euphoric and was tempted by the litre of Baileys in her bag, but thought better of it. At least she had George Michael for company, singing about 'Last Christmas', when she'd been doing exactly the same thing.

***

The next day was Christmas Eve and sure enough, true to Janet's word, the reindeer pen was empty. Not a Prancer or Vixen in sight. All eight deer were gone. Janet didn't seem unduly concerned. She spread the chewed carrot around the pen, proof that the herd had indeed eaten their last meal before flying off into the night sky with Father Christmas. She rubbed the small of her back as she stood upright and looked across to the tennis courts where a small figure was racing towards her, dragging the long-suffering Beth with him.

As he approached the fence, Santi checked his run to take in the sight of the vacant pen. He looked up at Janet and back into the pen.

"No way!"

"Way," replied Janet.

No more questions needed. Or so she thought.

"When will they be back?"

"When they've delivered all the presents."

As the word spread, kids and parents gathered by the fence and Janet held court once again, telling any and everyone that the reindeer had gone. She rushed around the pen like a pantomime dame, pretending to look for them, walking around the large oak tree, in the brambles at the side and behind the screens. She held her hands open as if to say, 'They've really gone'. And they really had gone, no two ways about it. The kids lapped it up and the parents were puzzled to say the least, which made it even more exciting. Everyone left the park that night feeling a bit more Christmassy than normal.

***

The Zoom call on Christmas Day to his grandparents in Lima was glitchy, but Santi didn't seem to notice, shouting and waving at his beloved *abuela*, telling her about the reindeer and how they were flying and delivering presents. Jose couldn't help but admire the absolute belief of his son and reached behind him in the drawer for his Christmas cigar.

***

It was Santi's greatest Christmas. He had loved the binoculars he'd got last year, and he would never forget the train set he'd got when he was five, but this year was on another level. Getting to know Janet, meeting the reindeer and witnessing with his own eyes how they had left the park to fly off and help Father Christmas deliver presents. Surely nothing was ever going to top this.

As Santi and Jose walked past Janet's hut, Santi thought of her at home and wondered what the reindeer had brought her. He had a little look through the window and saw three Christmas cards neatly arranged on the table.

Something stuck to Jose's foot, a scrunched-up A3 flier. He peeled it off and read the headline to himself:

NOTICE:
24th–26th DEC
REINDEER ABSENT FROM PARK
HOOF-ROT TREATMENT
ANY ENQUIRIES, PLEASE CONTACT
JANET ON 0207 3544778.

Santi looked up inquisitively.

"What is it, Papa?"

Jose paused for a moment and looked down at his beautiful boy. "It's nothing, Santi."

He gave Santi's hand a little squeeze and got a big one back.

***

Lloyd decided to do one last recce of the park before locking up. He was fine to work Christmas Day. He didn't have any family locally, so it wasn't like he was missing out on anything, plus he was paid double time, which was always welcome. And, if he was honest, it was possibly the easiest day of the year to work. Everyone was in a good mood, and most folks just wanted to stretch their legs and walk off their Christmas lunch.

He double-checked the ponds more out of habit than anything. Ever since seeing her skating all those months ago, he'd been drawn there most days, wondering if she'd ever return, or if she had been for real. He couldn't quite drag himself away, enjoying the feeling of being totally alone with her and the memory. The moment was broken by a moorhen squawking, trying to get settled in its nest. Lloyd smiled at his feathered friend, before peeling himself away and wandering back up to the main gates.

He took one last look across the park in the dwindling light, locked the gate and doffed his cap to Lord Clissold. "Merry Christmas, squire. Have a good one."

ACKNOWLEDGEMENTS

It's been quite a challenge to retrain my advertising brain to create longer rather than shorter content; to let ideas and characters breathe, instead of squeezing them into ever tighter spaces. But I've got the hang of it and here we are with fifty thousand words across nearly two hundred pages. What a luxury. For this I am indebted to a few people. Primarily my wife, Rachel. Thank you for listening to my ideas, nodding sagely at some and remaining stoically silent on others. Your patience, creativity and ability to spot sentences that aren't sentences have been fundamental in making this happen. Huge thanks also to Katy Darby who has been with me throughout the entire journey, first as my college tutor at City, University of London and then as editor guiding the stories and characters with brilliant direction. I want to also thank Gill Morton, Tom Campbell and Adam Leigh for their publishing advice, Kay Coleman for her cold read and warm encouragement, and, of course, Dave Buonaguidi aka The Real Hackney Dave for the wonderful front cover. Honourable mentions go to life-long friend Mick Greaney for his endless support, likewise Ben Kay in Los Angeles.

Finally, thank you to the locals: waggy-tailed ones in the form of Poppy and Eric, Ali and Yucel from the shop, my amazing daughters, Martha and Dorothy, and everyone who's frequented Clissold Park over the years. You've all played your part.

This book is printed on paper from sustainable sources managed under the Forest Stewardship Council (FSC) scheme.

It has been printed in the UK to reduce transportation miles and their impact upon the environment.

For every new title that Troubador publishes, we plant a tree to offset CO_2, partnering with the More Trees scheme.

For more about how Troubador offsets its environmental impact, see www.troubador.co.uk/sustainability-and-community